This man Slocum was a stranger. They'd just been introduced. She was another man's fiancée. She didn't know what made her do it.

She put her lips on his and her own kiss surprised her. He returned her kiss, open and seeking like her own.

"If they kill me right now," she said, "I couldn't be happier."

JAKE LOGAN

APACHE SUNRISE

BERKLEY BOOKS, NEW YORK

APACHE SUNRISE

A Berkley Book / published by arrangement with
the author

PRINTING HISTORY
Berkley edition / June 1983

ISBN: 0-425-06249-X

APACHE SUNRISE

1

The hand gripped the wooden slat of the cattle car. The slat had once been the bright red of the Denver Rio Grande Railroad, but the last time it was painted had been five years before, in 1876, and now the red was as dull as bloodstains. The slat was slivered and rough. The hand gripped all the tighter.

Just eight cattle cars in the train, plus the long passenger coach at the tail end for the troopers. The engine was a 2-4-4-2, capable of pulling much heavier loads, and it traveled along at a pretty good clip.

Once past the Sierras, the train hit speeds of nearly eighty miles an hour howling across the great plains: the black locomotive, the blur of faded red, the brass-and-blue of the troop car. The locomotive had a good boiler and an enormous tender, so it skipped two out of every three water stops, hooting through towns and way stations alike, cinders blowing about, the suck of its passing making wind in the still Kansas air.

The semaphore was always green. The train blasted past freight trains, mail trains, even a couple of the long transcontinental expresses, sidetracked to make way.

It hadn't even been ten years since the southern transcontinental rail link had been joined, but passengers on the southern route took fast transport for granted and many of them grumbled as they waited for the special train to come through.

1

"Damned inconsiderate, if you ask me. I heard it was an army train. I don't see why we should have to wait for a bunch of soldier boys to go by."

"They said it wasn't soldier boys, Henry. They said it was special."

"Well, it's a shame, I tell you." Cutting the tip off a cigar, the man blew a plume of smoke at the parlor-car ceiling and looked at the wasteland around them, the rough, endless country shimmering in the September sun.

"They said it wouldn't be long."

And, sure enough, the special train whooshed through the switch, the cars shaking from side to side on their trucks, the wheels screeching against the rails.

"Lord almighty! Did you see that thing? I believe that train was doing better than a mile a minute."

"It was fast, Henry. Mighty fast. What were those? Cattle cars? I think I saw one of the cowboys' hands."

"Cowpuncher, dear. The men who ride inside with the cows—they call them cowpunchers."

"Thank you, Henry."

Swaying, hurling itself against the curves, the train roared east. By morning, near Gainesville, it crossed the Mississippi on the tremendous wooden trestle. As the wheels drummed against the wooden planks a great flock of wild ducks rose from the estuary beneath and soared up past the windows.

There were fifty soldiers crammed into the one forty-foot coach. Their five officers had commandeered the first third of the coach, swiveled the seats into double beds, and put their legs up. The other men slept three to a seat or sprawled in the aisles. The rifles and sabers made it more awkward. A man could hardly stroll to the back platform to take a leak without knocking someone else's saber onto the floor, and each pilgrimage to the rear was accompanied by curses.

The soldiers carried everything with them except water. Their rations were hardtack and beans, carried in their own haversacks. Those who were awake filled their canteens at the infrequent water stops.

Twenty-five men, half the force, were awakened when the locomotive started clanging the water signal. They grumbled and cursed and kicked each other and gathered by the front and rear of the coach.

"Each man check the weapon of the man beside him. I want every man's Spencer with a round in the chamber but, by God, I'll flog the man who has his cocked."

The noncoms pressed through the crowd to get to the doors and the locomotive hooted then—one, two, three—the agreed-upon signal.

"Steady, men. Steady now."

The noncoms tensed when they heard the squeal as the driving wheels reversed and the couplings smashed together and jolted sleepers awake. The noncoms gripped the door frames until their knuckles turned white and the two lieutenants called out unnecessary orders that couldn't be heard anyway because of the screech of the wheels.

Men stood shoulder to shoulder, pressed against each other in an unwanted intimacy that created more harsh curses, shoves, and a few threats.

"You son of a bitch! Step on my toe one more time and I'll make your wife a widow."

"Go to hell, you ignorant bastard."

Outside the ground rushed by, slower, slower, until the first noncom launched himself out. Quick as a pile of falling cordwood, his men and officers followed behind.

Before the locomotive was completely stopped, they were dogtrotting forward, carbines at the trail, in two files, one on each side of the train. By the numbers, they flopped down then, odds and evens. The odd-numbered men faced the dusty red cattle cars, rifles at their shoulders. The even-numbered men faced outward, their eyes seeking the rescuers nobody expected to see.

Silence. The stretch of the undulant plain. A few scrub cattle grazing on a distant knoll. The empty road that wound toward the water stop. A couple of citizens waiting for the morning milk train into Wichita.

"Now, what the hell? What the hell? This is a public place, isn't it? Don't you be pushin' at me, soldier boy."

"Sorry, sir. We just can't have anyone get close to the train. Just following orders."

"Well, what you want me and the missus to do? Stand back here in the road? And what about our luggage?"

"Nobody'll touch your bags," the boyish lieutenant said with a smile. The lieutenant couldn't have been more than twenty, not three years out of the Point, fair-haired and blue-eyed. Only the long, narrow scar across his right cheek dispelled the illusion of boyishness.

The passengers for the milk train moved back, grumbling, but took places where they could keep an eye on their humble possessions.

"We'll only be a few minutes," the lieutenant called. "Just enough time to fill the water tank."

"What's that smell, soldier boy? My God, that stink's enough to gag a maggot!"

The lieutenant ignored the question. The train crew had lowered the long goosenecked nozzle into the boiler and the water was rushing into the tender. The tender had been full of coal when the trip started. It was no more than a quarter full now. Coal-fired locomotives were rather rare in the West, and the lieutenant hoped the railroad had made provisions for a coaling stop before they were dead empty. He'd hate like hell to have to wait in some godforsaken place for more coal.

The hand held the slat of the cattle car as it had for two days and one night, since the train loaded in Socorro, New Mexico. The hand held a slat halfway up the car, about five and a half feet from the car's floor. It had four rather small brown fingers and a long, slender thumb with a crooked scar on its back. The nails were long, broken, and dirty. One nail was torn off and the newer, pinker skin beneath pulsed with life. The soldiers hardly noticed the hand. They'd seen it at every stop and had long ago stopped wondering whose it was.

"It's a wonder they don't choke on their own stink," one private remarked. "Lord, how can human beings live like that?"

"Quiet on the line!" their sergeant shouted. "I want a detail of three men to fill canteens. Murphy, that's you. Maxwell, Pusey. Any man got to take a crap, you just let me know and I'll relieve you while you go behind the tower."

A carefully disguised voice said, "Sergeant, I'll go anywhere with you."

"You shut up down there. Damn it! I will have some order here!"

They were not garrison troops. They wore the distinctive facings and blouses of Crook's Fifth Cavalry, United States Army. Many of them had fought beside Custer in the Washita eight years earlier, and a few of them had served with Reno on that fateful day in 1876 when five troops of the Seventh Cavalry discovered immortality courtesy of Sitting Bull, war chief and shaman of the Sioux nation.

Sitting Bull was shut up safe now, a prisoner on the Pine Ridge reservation. Crazy Horse, the best of his subchiefs, had been dead for four years. Chief Joseph, Black Kettle, White Cloud, Roman Nose— they were all good Indians now, thanks to these pony soldiers and men just like them.

The men who rode under Crook and Howard and Custer were roughnecks, barely-literate immigrants, dirt poor. In 1881, their officers weren't awfully much better. The few chances for advancement in the United States Army were taken by those who stayed close to Washington and the War Department, not the soldiers who rode out after Indians, a thankless, inglorious, and frequently fatal choice.

They had been molded into one of the toughest fighting organizations the world had ever seen. They might sign the pay roster with an X, but the Spencers tucked under their arms were immaculate and each man had either honed his action or traded a plug of tobacco to the big Swede in D Company who, everybody knew, had a real knack for gunsmithing. They might have made lousy hus-

bands and worse fathers but their sabers were sharp
enough to shave with and most of them had been
blooded more than once. The officers might be young
and unpromising, without the powerful connections
that could have kept them closer to the War Department, but these downy-cheeked youngsters had time
and again faced the wiliest, most ruthless opponents
and brought them to heel. The men were veterans,
and generally pretty easy with each other.

Among the men facing those silent, rust-red cattle
cars, more than a few had their thumbs hooked
around the hammers. And the men so nervously
handling their weapons, so primed to cock and fire,
weren't the newest men among them; they were the
most experienced and the most practical.

The best men of these crack troops were jittery.

The doors were sealed with the same heavy lead
War Department seal that fastened payroll strongboxes
and shipments of important documents. The single
protruding hand was the only sign of human life. No
sound came from those cars louder than the constant
buzzing of the flies, but an observer might have
noticed that every noncom outside the train stood
with his pistol holster unfastened and the flap tucked
back, and nobody took his eyes off those cars for
very long.

The engineer tooted the five-minute warning. Two
officers and a sergeant crawled underneath the cattle
cars, checking for broken planks. The floorboards
were three-inch white pine, strong and rough, and
the occupants of the cattle cars had no steel to cut
with. But these soldiers hadn't reached their present
age by carelessness. The careless among them were

long dead, buried in hurriedly dug, shallow graves beside this water hole or that forgotten encampment.

The colonel commanding the detachment had fought under Grant at the Wilderness seventeen years before. Seventeen years since the slow pressure of U. S. Grant's will broke the back of the Confederacy. The colonel had been a young officer then. He wouldn't get his lieutenancy until the siege of Petersburg.

The colonel was in charge of four lieutenants and fifty soldiers. He had never looked inside the cars, and hadn't wanted to. The manifest made him personally responsible for thirty-four women, seventeen children, and fourteen men, plus, of course, "Himself." Well, if fifty men of the Fifth Cavalry couldn't handle this job, nobody could.

Still, the colonel would be a little happier once his part of it was ended.

"Himself" had broken a few careers: pushed generals into premature retirements, changed captains into lieutenants, and hastened more than a few honest soldiers into early graves.

The colonel snapped his orders and, after the noncoms finished crawling around the rusty cattle cars, he got down on his hands and knees and checked what they had already checked.

Beneath the car where he'd seen the hand, he heard a chuckle. No way of telling who that hand belonged to, but there was no doubt about the chuckle—light, musical, amused, almost feminine. The colonel came out on the other side of the cattle car, beat the dust off his knees, and wondered how many men had been escorted out of this life by that delighted, cheerful, murderous chuckle.

The colonel waved his campaign hat and the engineer tooted in response. The great driving wheels of the locomotive spun against the track and took hold.

The colonel swung aboard the car. Rank has its privileges—in this case, nothing more than a double seat for himself and plenty of space for his luggage. He buckled and flapped his holster before he sat down. Like his men, the colonel had been ready.

Five hours before the next water stop. He checked his written itinerary. That would be in Alabama, a town called Dothan. And the next stop would be in Florida.

The hand clung to the slat as the train dove into the late-summer lushness of an Alabama night. The moon was full. From time to time, above the hand, something shone between the slats in the moonlight, like a cat's eyes caught in lamplight or the red glare of a mockingbird's eyes.

The moon splashed its light on the twin silver rails, the white gravel roadbed, the dark locomotive, and the racing cars. Five or ten minutes after the locomotive passed, the calls of the night birds and the singing of the frogs would resume.

Fireflies blinked. The hand did not relax its grasp. When the water signal sounded, the hand stayed wrapped around that slat, just as it had been for two and a half days.

It was three A.M., the hour when sentries fall asleep at their post, the hour when a crawling man startles ground-nesting birds aloft, the hour for stealth. The eyes above the hand watched as the noncoms kicked their troopers into wakefulness. The eyes watched the troops lie down and take aim. "Himself" watched the nervous ones with their nervous fingers. A conical Spencer bullet would pass through the side of this cattle car as if it were made of reeds. Through the slats, through the humans inside, and, likely, out the other side. If "Himself" had had his wish, he would have wished the firing to commence right away.

A voice came to his ear from the darkness—a woman's voice, filled with terror and hopelessness. Sharply, he rebuked her.

The woman withdrew. Since she could not wail aloud, she wailed in silence, and in silence the others in the car wailed with her.

The colonel stood behind his men at each stop, and perhaps he was the first to hear the hoofbeats of the racing brougham. It was all black and black horses drew it. Their bits and bridles gleamed like pale stars in the moonlight.

"Officers, look to your men!"

The tension rippled down the prone men like a wave.

The fair-haired lieutenant intercepted the brougham at the platform of the little station. "Sorry, sir, but . . ."

The brougham's only passenger had a telegram for the colonel commanding the special detachment, Fifth Cavalry, Dothan, Alabama. "This is Dothan sure enough. Are you the colonel?"

"You just wait here in case there's some reply."

WAR DEPARTMENT ORDERS YOU TO SIDING AT DOTHAN UNTIL FURTHER ORDERS

The telegram was signed by a general the colonel knew and respected. The colonel supposed they were waiting for coal; he couldn't think of any other reason for a delay.

After the trainmen threw the infrequently used switches, the massive locomotive pulled its light train onto a brushy siding which wound off among the trees until it was quite out of sight of the water tower and the tiny station.

The colonel looked at the telegram again and shrugged. He ordered the dusty red cars to be pulled under the shade of some kind of thick, unfamiliar trees. They were tulip trees, but the colonel never knew that.

The soldiers were glad enough to get out of the cramped coach and the officers arranged guard duty in shifts. The colonel detailed pickets and let most of his grateful troops sleep.

The temperature climbed into the nineties the next morning. Despite the shade of the tulip trees, by noon the metalwork on the locomotive was too hot to touch and a man standing on the iron couplings could feel the heat through his boot soles. Bottle flies, greenflies, bloat flies, horseflies, sweat bees, and mosquitoes swarmed in and out of the slats. Several of the mosquitoes landed on the protruding hand, drew blood, and flew on, staggered by their load.

The air was thick and hard to breathe. The troopers were used to heat, but the humidity made a man feel like he was half underwater, drowning in the air.

The lieutenant who took over at noon had his men pull back another fifty feet from the cars. The smell had grown worse: urine, feces, death.

The colonel picked a runner. "You get on into town. I want a message sent."

The telegram he sent read:

PRISONERS DYING IN HEAT STOP NO
WATER FOOD THREE DAYS STOP ADVISE

The runner sent his message and waited three
hours for a reply.

The telegraph key started chattering.

IMMEDIATELY PROCEED ORLANDO
YARDS AWAIT FURTHER ORDERS.

The order was signed by the same general.

The colonel hesitated. Though the sun was low,
the heat hadn't lessened, inside those cars—well, it
didn't do the stomach good to have a too-active
imagination. Perhaps he should let them out, water
them. Horses and mules died on a transcontinental
trip without water.

But the telegram had said immediately, and the
colonel was three short years from retirement.

The locomotive had never lost its pressure. It was
the work of minutes for it to build up a full head of
steam. Once more the troopers boarded their cramped
coach. The driving wheels squealed their eagerness
and the train backed out of the siding and onto the
main line.

Inside the train, the colonel showed his telegram
to both lieutenants. If he arrived with a damaged
cargo, he wanted witnesses.

The train rolled southeast and entered the plateau
of central Florida, passing lush savannas, groves of
scrub oak and Osage orange. It was cattle country
here. The locomotive's headlamp lit up cows beside
the tracks.

The humidity didn't improve and it was a terrible effort, sometimes, to draw breath.

At dawn they reached Orlando where they were signaled into another siding, the farthest from the station. The station was a rather elaborate tile-and-brick affair with minarets.

The underbrush came down to the train on both sides and was impenetrable. The colonel stationed his men on the roadbed, where they had a field of fire up and down the track. The stench from those cars was appalling. The hand which gripped the slat was swollen, the knuckles nearly invisible.

This close the soldiers couldn't help seeing between the slats. Dim shapes huddled on the floors, lined with narrow, interrupted bands of light. The white gravel roadbed shimmered in the heat. The soldiers were beyond complaining. They were irritable, blind with discomfort, and would have killed for some real shade and an ice-cold drink of water.

The colonel expected somebody to be waiting in Orlando, but he had no such luck. Now the colonel expected somebody to arrive at any minute. Thinking like that took until noon, when the sun stood directly overhead and the railroad men got underneath the locomotive tender and lay down, panting like dogs.

Because of the stink, the soldiers breathed through their mouths and conversations were adenoidal.

The colonel finally figured out a way to water his charges. He'd have his men pour their canteens through the slats, hoping to find open mouths on the far side. He wouldn't need to break the seals, and his prisoners would live. Surely the War Department wanted them to live!

The colonel thought over his decision. He looked at it on all sides. By one P.M., when he was ready to give the order, a trainman came hurrying down the track. He wore the high-collared vested suit of a conductor.

"Colonel!" he called. "Where's the colonel in command?"

The colonel swung down from the car and waited, hands on his hips. The trainman picked him out. "There's a special express gonna be backing onto this siding directly. What's that awful smell? What you hauling back there—dead swine?"

"What special?"

The trainman turned to indicate the observation platform creeping toward them. "That special, Colonel. I've got my signals to do. You just warn your men and I'll be about my business."

The trainman unfurled his flag and guided the new train until its rear clicked against the troop car.

The special's observation car was a dark, lustrous green with brass handles, brass railings, and the single letter "W" in brass dead center on the observation platform.

After a few minutes, the rear door opened and a portly man came out wearing a dressing gown and smoking a long, narrow cigar. "Colonel Bagnel, I assume?" he said.

The colonel checked his salute. "Sir, you have the advantage of me."

"Welfleet. Abel Welfleet. Senator Abel Welfleet of Illinois."

So the colonel executed his salute after all. "Perhaps you can enlighten me, sir, as to this delay. My prisoners . . ."

The portly man smiled. "Getting a trifle thirsty, are they? A trifle hot? My God, this is hot country, Colonel. We have nothing like this in Illinois."

"Sir, if I don't get some water to them I fear there'll be fatal consequences."

The senator sniffed the air like a man sampling fine wine. "Smells like there have already been a few fatal consequences, Colonel."

"Senator, I have women and children on this train."

"No, sir," the portly man snapped, "you do not. You have Apaches on this train. Chiricahuas, I believe. Brutes—savages."

"Brutes and savages need water, too, Senator."

The senator beamed at him, as if they were the very best of old friends. "Yes, sir—and they shall have it. But first, why don't you come inside out of this blasted heat? I have some chilled Monopole and some cold meats laid on for luncheon. Will you join me?"

So the two men ate a leisurely meal while the sun heated the roof of the troop car so badly nobody remained inside. The Apaches, of course, remained inside their cars. They had no choice.

After their meal, the two men talked. The senator showed the colonel a letter from the War Department, authored by that same general the colonel had soldiered with so many years before. The letter gave the senator complete authority with regard to the Apache captives scheduled to be transported to Fort Pensacola. They were his to do with as he pleased.

And what he pleased was that the colonel should line up his men on the outside of the train and break the War Department seals.

Every one of the fifty troopers took his position, rifle at the ready, while a noncom smashed the seals and slid the slatted doors open.

Behind the semicircle of troopers, the senator and the colonel stood quite comfortably with the air of well-fed men of good conscience.

"I wish to speak to Geronimo!" the senator shouted.

The hand unclasped and withdrew itself inside. In a moment, a figure appeared in the doorway. A slight figure, no more than five and a half feet tall, yet he seemed taller. His moccasins were calf-high, his legs bare above them. He wore a leather breech-clout and a long, tunic-like leather overshirt that came down below his waist and was belted by a wide leather belt studded with silver Mexican pesos. He wore a bright kerchief at his throat and his head was bare.

"I am Geronimo."

Though the senator wasn't really aware of speaking, the colonel heard him say, "Damn, what a proud bastard."

Calmly, Geronimo surveyed his captors. He might have been the President about to make a speech instead of a captive under their guns. He stretched slowly, raising his hands over his head in some ancient obeisance to the cruel sun.

"Are your people thirsty?" The senator cried out the question.

Geronimo watched a snowy egret sail past the train, high against the sky. He scratched himself absently.

"Do your people thirst?" the senator repeated. "Would they like to get out of the cars?"

Geronimo moved his black eyes over the assembled white men, seeking the speaker. Every man touched by those diamond-hard eyes winced a bit. "My people are Apaches," he said. He made to spit his contempt, but couldn't find enough moisture in his mouth. Without asking permission, he jumped down from the car and strolled toward the waiting officers.

The senator lost a little of the red from his complexion.

"Steady," the colonel commanded.

Up and down the line the men cocked their hammers.

Geronimo smiled. The smile was vaguely paternal, as if the soldiers were children who had learned their lessons well.

"Stop, or you're a dead man!" the colonel shouted.

Still smiling that smile, Geronimo took three or four more steps before he stopped. "Now," he said. "Now I can see your eyes."

And, as the Indian spoke, the senator's eyes felt curiously exposed, more looked at than looking; as though by possessing them he was more vulnerable. "We must talk," he said, and his mouth felt dry as dust.

"Sergeant," the colonel snapped. "The irons."

The senator looked his question.

"Standing orders, sir. Any time he is out of that car, he's to wear leg irons," said the colonel.

"I have worn them before," Geronimo said. "No," he went on. "You kill me this time."

The two noncoms bearing their heavy, clanking burden stopped short. This was truly an impasse. The senator coughed and hid his face in his hands.

"Let the Apaches out of the cars," he said. "Let them have water. Take a squad of men and wash the cars down. It must be filthy in there."

The colonel didn't want to do it and kept refusing until the angry senator scribbled a direct order on a page from his memo book. "There, damn your eyes! Do as I have said!"

The Apaches filed out of the cars very slowly. The bucks were extremely weak, the women more so. Most of the children were in the adults' arms. When they were laid down beside the cars, they resembled cordwood more than children. Eleven of them were dead.

"Geronimo!" the senator cried out. "I have come to help your people." His sweeping gesture included the dead children.

It had been the senator who had delayed the train. It had been the senator who had decreed the cars should be sealed until the train reached its destination. Though part of his mind knew this perfectly well, he was still able to crank up his indignation. The army has killed your people. I wish only to help."

Geronimo's face was impassive. He seemed to have come through the ordeal better than most. Two of his warriors tottered over to stand at his side. His black eyes never wavered.

"Who are his family?" the senator whispered in the colonel's ear.

"That wench over there is one of his wives," the colonel said.

"Put two guards on her. Bring her to me."

At the colonel's command, two soldiers rushed to the dull-eyed Indian woman and dragged her before the colonel. The riflemen watched Geronimo for any sign of a reaction but he crossed his arms and craned his neck around, searching the sky for another white bird, perhaps envying their simple, inhuman freedom.

"Geronimo, I wish to offer you much. I wish to ask your counsel. I wish to be your friend," the senator declared.

"This is why you hold my woman?" Geronimo shrugged. "It is a strange act of friendship. But if you—the white man—say it is friendship, then I must believe you." He spoke quite seriously, but he was mocking them, and they knew it.

The woman sagged between the soldiers. She had once been a comely Indian girl, just sixteen years old. She was still only sixteen years old, but she was neither plump nor comely. A string of drool at the corner of her mouth and the pallor of her skin showed the effects of serious heat exhaustion. The woman was in shock. She didn't know who held her.

"I would help your wife." To the colonel, the senator said, "Get some water into this girl. Get her cooled down. If any soldier molests her, I'll make sure the only retirement he ever knows is at Leavenworth."

As the colonel gave his orders, Geronimo asked politely, "Will you help my wife like you have helped my other wives?" He pointed at the row of dead children. "Like you have helped my son?"

The senator was startled, but he hadn't attained his present prominence through slow wits. He turned to the colonel. "I told you to treat them well, and you did not. This death is on your conscience."

The colonel sighed. "Senator," he noted, "they're just Apaches."

"You did not wish this to happen?" Geronimo asked the senator.

The senator sensed an opening through which the two of them could communicate. "No," he said. "I did not wish the Apaches to suffer."

"And you are the chief of these men?" Genuine puzzlement showed in the Indian's voice and face.

"I am their chief." Senator Welfleet tapped his chest.

"You are a very weak chief if they do not do as you wish," Geronimo said. He yawned. "You whites have killed four of my wives and more sons than I wish to count. Why should you think one more death matters to me?"

The senator's jaw dropped. There was a moment of calm: the ready soldiers, the Indians collapsed, or the next thing to it. It was as though the slight, bareheaded figure was of some alien race, neither Indian nor white—something quite different.

The senator had hoped to take Geronimo easily, with no investment on his part. If that was not to be, he was realistic enough to change courses. "Forget the leg irons," he said. "Get them some water. Set out a detail to bury the bodies. I want them well buried." To Geronimo he said simply, "Come," and turned his back and mounted the steps of his own private car, leaving the door open as invitation.

The Indian deliberated for a minute before he followed.

Inside the cool car Geronimo found the senator seated at a linen-covered table, the same sort of table the white eyes used for their lying treaties. A beautiful glass decanter held half a gallon of cool water.

The senator filled both glasses and gestured for the Indian to drink.

Geronimo stayed on his feet. The water that might have soothed his cracked and bleeding lips remained on the table. The Indian almost swayed. Almost.

"I ordered that your people should suffer," the senator admitted. "I wished to weaken your will."

"And have you weakened it?" The Apache's voice was as breathless as a dying sigh.

"I have work for you. Your kind of work."

"The white eye has work for me? A purpose? I have no more land to cede. My Chiricahuas are helpless in your hands."

"Ah, yes." The senator was pleased at this belated admission. "Have some water."

The Indian licked his cracked lips. "I have already had too much water. I am awash with your kind of water."

"Sit down."

The Indian remained standing.

"Sit down and I'll tell you how you and your people can win your freedom." The senator hadn't planned to offer so much so soon, but Geronimo's pride left him little choice.

Geronimo sat. He lifted the glass of water to the light and delighted in its reflections. Very slowly, smiling at the senator's face, he poured the water onto the genuine turkestan carpet. He replaced the upended glass in the exact spot it had occupied when full. "I wonder how you will die," he said conversationally. "I should like to try you. I think after several hours you would beg me. I think you would offer me anything, even the heart of your mother and father, if I would stop what I was doing."

The senator wiped perspiration from his forehead and drank most of his water in one long gulp. Nervously he opened the leather folder before him. He paraphrased from the extremely detailed report prepared for the War Department. "You were born in 1829—some think 1830. A subchief under Cochise and Mangus Colorado. When Mangus Colorado died . . ."

"He was murdered by your white soldiers. His murder was the greatest wrong that has been done to the Apaches."

Airily, the senator waved it away. "Your first wife and child were killed by Mexican soldiers and you've been at war ever since. You and your warriors have killed hundreds of white settlers, scores of soldiers, and nobody knows how many Mexican troops and civilians. When Crook brought you in, many officers wanted you tried for murder."

"Murder?"

"You have killed very many men and women, too, who meant you no harm."

"Meant me no harm?" Geronimo laughed. He pulled that laugh from the depths of his belly and shook it until the room rattled. "Which white man means Geronimo no harm?" His smile invited complicity, requested an answer.

"*I* mean you no harm."

"My dead son will be glad to know you mean us no harm. It is a thing I do not understand. If you kill us, why not say you kill us? I have killed very many of your pony soldiers. Some with these bare hands." Geronimo held his hands before the senator's face. The senator winced. He wished he'd thought to leave a couple of windows open. The inside of his private car was beginning to smell.

"How many of your warriors can still fight?" the senator asked brusquely.

"Those who still live."

Exasperated, the senator set down his pen. He was tired of this man's bullying ways. "How many of your warriors can ride a horse and do harm to their enemies?"

Geronimo held up one hand this time and flicked all five fingers three times. "That many."

"Would you like to be free?"

Geronimo looked away. When those eyes left his, the senator felt how much power they had. *Why,* he thought, *if this man were white he'd be one of our greatest* . . . He couldn't complete the thought. *Generals? Presidents?*

Geronimo took up his glass again.

"Ah. Just so." The senator rubbed his hands together. "I suppose you know what we intend for the Apaches?"

Geronimo gripped the glass.

"The army means to take you to Fort Pensacola, where you will farm the land like white men. You will walk in the furrows behind the plow and your women will stay in their huts. You will wear white men's clothing and eat our foods. We will train you to constant labor for no reward. We will give you no horses except plow horses and no weapons to kill your enemies. You will be protected by sloppy garrison troops who will pay your women to sleep with them. Your children will grow up as white children and go to white schools and forget the Apache language and Apache ways."

Geronimo laughed. "And you call us savages because we take three days to torture an enemy. You would take many years to torture, and your enemy's children are not safe from you. But yours is the civilized way." Dramatically he clasped his own chest. "Teach me, white man, that I may become civilized."

"Are you ready for water?"

Geronimo looked at his empty glass. "You offer my people freedom?"

"I do."

"And will you make your promise like all white men make their promises? Do you write the treaty only to break it?"

"I will set your warriors free to do what is needed. I will set them free under your command this afternoon. When you are successful, I will set your women free as well. You shall not go to Florida. You will return to the mountains you love."

"And be hunted down by the army?"

Now it was the senator's turn to smile. "That will be between you and the army. Once you are free in your own country, you may do what you wish."

"And if I'm taken again?"

"You'll learn to love Florida. It's such a pleasant climate for someone who's used to the mountains and the arid plateaus."

"You are not to be my friend."

"A white man can do business with anyone. We do not have to be friends."

Geronimo was more puzzled by this than by anything that had gone before. "I am to be your friend, to do what you wish, yet you are not to be my friend. How can that be?"

"You kill a man for me and I'll set you free in your home country. That's my offer. You'll probably die out there, you and your whole damn tribe, but I'll put you there. That is my promise."

Geronimo looked at him for a very long time, weighing his words. Geronimo had heard many white men's promises. This one differed from the others in that it had limitations. What did this man offer him except a chance to die in his homeland? "You may pour me some water," he said. "I'm very thirsty."

Slowly, carefully, the senator poured until the water ran over the glass, filling the glass, spilling over the tablecloth, emptying the pitcher as if it was the bottomless well of generosity, of wealth beyond imagining.

2

When you've got just one hour to live, you might as well spend it like the hours that went before. No sense spending your last hour repenting. That was how John Slocum figured it, anyway.

"Preacher," he said, "get the hell out of my cell. I seen vultures that looked like you before, but they had more discriminating appetites." He tipped his hat over his eyes.

The preacher stepped back.

Lying on the bunk, the murderer, John Slocum, had enough power to put fear in a man. Slocum was a tall man. His boots hung over the jailhouse bunk by a good six inches. His hair was black as the underside of a raven's wing. His jaw was long and some might call it cruel. His eyes—well, the preacher was glad for Slocum's hat. He never felt comfortable staring into those strange, mocking green eyes. Cat's eyes—a wildcat's eyes.

Those eyes would be closed soon enough. The preacher pulled his repeater from his vest pocket and checked it. Fifty-four minutes to go.

Though the man hadn't stirred from his place on the bunk, somehow he'd seen the move. "You in a hurry, preacher?"

"No, no, no." He spoke too nervously, too swiftly. And he felt rather than saw the prisoner's grin. It wasn't right. The preacher had come to console many a poor pilgrim in his last hour on earth and he'd never seen one like this one before. Why, the man was positively . . . insolent.

"Preacher, since you're gonna stay here until I'm dead meat, why don't you be of some use? You go to the window there and stick your head up to the bars. You're a lanky bastard. Get up on your tiptoes and tell me about my crowd. I hope I drew a good crowd."

The window was a narrow slit cut deep through the thick walls of the jailhouse. The jail itself was set about halfway up the slope of the town they had named in honor of the dead bird found sprawled out on a rock when the first French Canadian trader set up his trading post here. Gull, Dakota Territory, was midway between the railhead and end of track. It had formerly been a trading post, and a jumping-off point for wagon trains on the cold northern route through the Dakotas. And it had been the end of track, for it was here that Jay Nelsh's Great Northern had paused briefly, gathering strength, scarce money, and energy to hurl itself farther across the barren Dakotas.

Gull had water. At the bottom of the jailhouse slope a thin, weary tributary of the Milk River curled and moped along. It was never deep and it never ran clear and some men swore they had to strain the water through the gaps in their teeth. But it was water, and in this part of the Dakotas, just a hundred miles east of the badlands, water was frighteningly scarce.

The ranchers who ran Texas cows on the free range near here were the backbone of the town. Here they bought salt blocks, harness buckles, ax heads, gunpowder, and tobacco. And, now, here they'd

ship their cows. Already a consortium had built a
complete stockyard: loading chutes, corrals, and all.
The stockyard was so new its unpainted pine was
still yellow. It hadn't been so awfully long since the
railroad tracks came through—not six months. Nelsh,
who had his railhead farther east in Fargo, would
move to Gull in the spring. The merchants of Gull
were pleased, thinking to enjoy some of the prosperity they deserved.

Perhaps that desire for prosperity had insured John
Slocum's demise, or perhaps it was no more than the
town's desire to appear respectable. Hell, the smoke
hadn't all dribbled out of the muzzle of Slocum's
Colt before they had him up before a judge in a
hastily convened court held in the big storeroom of
Arnie Nelson's Mercantile. The judge, after a short
speech on the march of law, convicted Slocum
in record time. Hell, that was just last week,
and they had the gallows built in three days flat,
which was fair speed for a real trapdoor gallows with
sandbag counterweights and a lever for the hangman
to trip. The lever was almost as tall as a man. Of
course, once a man went through the trap, he'd be
taller, too.

John Slocum had been in trouble most of his years
as a man but the speed of this trouble had really
surprised him. Hell, he'd done no more than anyone
would have done. How was he to guess that they'd
want to string him up?

"Any women out there in the crowd?" he asked.

The crowd's murmurings and calls sounded loud
as an ocean beyond the jailhouse walls.

"I see a few matrons," the preacher replied. "One
or two girl children here to enjoy the spectacle. Of

course, there are a few sisters who are no better than they should be."

"Uh-huh. Tell me about those."

"Who?"

"The whores, you dimwit. What do you think I'd have to do with matrons or girl children?"

"Then you are not a married man?"

Though Slocum had been married once—God, was it as long ago as that?—he didn't want this preacher walking around in his memories, and he lied. "No." And mentally asked Bird Walking, his slain Blackfoot wife, to forgive him.

Then he got to thinking about her and how it had been that one cold winter on the Tongue River. His heart fell and he began to feel that it wasn't such a bad idea that they hang him. He didn't have all that much to live for.

"The painted women are in a surrey and they are behaving shamelessly with the men who accost them."

John Slocum closed his eyes to see them better. The red-fringed surrey, drawn by two bone-white carriage horses—Morgans, they were, though how two of that new breed got all the way out here to Dakota Territory was too much to guess. The girls would be wearing wraps: some plush velvet, some lace, to protect them against the bite which early in September everybody could feel in the air. They'd be accepting kisses on the hand from their admirers, but nothing more serious. Just raising up the natural curiosity of a man, making themselves mysterious who were so free and easy back home at the Abilene House.

"I don't suppose there's a yellow-haired woman among them? Young woman, nineteen at best."

"I can't . . . Yes. Seated in the back between two of her sisters. She appears to be crying."

"Well, that's some comfort, at least." Slocum grinned to himself. Of all the people in the wide, wide world, none would mourn him except one young whore. And she'd forget him soon as another couple thousand men had taken rest between her thighs.

It hadn't started out that way. Before the War, he'd been just another farmer's son in the mountains of western Georgia. Over a thousand acres, about a quarter of it cropland, the rest pastureland or woodlot. Slocum's Stand. That's what they'd called the place ever since John Slocum's great-great-great grand-daddy first put down stakes, armed with a Kentucky long rifle, some geegaws to hold the Indians off his back, and a scrap of paper from King George saying he owned this little piece of land. It would have been easier on great-great-great grandpap if the Indians could read, but they couldn't, and they took the man's scalp. His son held the land, and every Slocum thereafter had been born in the big old brick farmhouse. Cattle, sheep, and hogs. Corn for feed, corn for whiskey. They even had their own little gristmill down by Chilly Draft, the stream that ran below the hayfields. John Slocum and his brother Robert planned to run the place together when their time came.

Their time came before they were quite ready for it, when South Carolina seceded from the Union, followed in rapid succession by the other states that were to become the Confederate States of America.

Robert was posted to a Cavalry outfit, a division commanded by one George Pickett. John Slocum had always been a fine hand with a squirrel rifle, and the sharpshooter's weapon fit his shoulder just as snugly as the squirrel gun had.

He commanded a small detachment of sharpshooters on Little Round Top. From there he watched as General Pickett threw away his division on that terrible charge through the peach orchard. John Slocum kept his rifle smoking, dropping one Yankee officer after another, firing until his rifle got hot. Later they called it the highwater mark of the Confederacy, where those few survivors broke through the Union lines so briefly. John Slocum always remembered it as a turkey shoot. The rifle hot in his hands, the sights wavering in the heat waves off the barrel as he sought the gold braid of officer's rank. He never was to know how many men he killed that day.

That night, walking the battlefield by lantern light, he found his brother, who'd never know any more about anything. At least he had died quickly. The moans of the badly hurt around him, their whimpers and cries, allowed John Slocum to take some real comfort in his brother's rapid death.

The cholera took his mother and father too, while he was riding with the army of the Trans-Mississippi. General Shelby had offered to let him go home, but from the date on the letter, he figured they'd be long buried. The general was really offering him a chance to desert and young John Slocum knew it. Desert and spend the last few months of the war on his family farm, complete with the papers to keep him safe from the Confederate Army's increasingly desperate conscriptions.

"No, Sir," young Slocum had said. "I've nothing to look for at home."

He spent the last days of the War in terrible danger and even took a bullet which almost killed him. When the young ex-Captain of the Confederate States of America finally rode home in the spring of 1866 he found a run-down, neglected farm with no livestock, no small tools, and no furniture. The spring-house was still standing and the big barn, too. With a little work—a lot of back-breaking work—a man—a crazy man—could make something out of Slocum's Stand. It already was something: a ruin.

So he set to. He never wanted much more than the next man. A home, an honorable livelihood, a wife, kids, a fast horse to ride on Saturday night, and a quiet soul.

That wasn't the way it happened. A man thought Slocum's Stand would make an ideal small horse farm. The man was one of the breed of men they were already beginning to call carpetbaggers. They were the occupation authority in a conquered nation. This particular carpetbagger wanted Slocum's Stand enough to try to steal it, along with his hired gun.

They weren't much of a match for the plow boy who suddenly turned terrible with his old Colt Navy smoking in his hand. John Slocum planted both of them which, all things considered, wasn't such a red-hot idea, since the carpetbagger was a federal judge. Judges don't like it when somebody starts burying judges before their time. When John Slocum left his home county, troops and warrants pursued him.

He might have made a good life in Georgia. Years later, in the Wind River Mountains with Bird Walking and their infant son, he gave it another try. While he was away on a hunting trip, an army trader sold her a genuine three-beaver Hudson's Bay blanket, as beautiful as it was deadly. The army had wrapped the bodies of smallpox victims in their beautiful blankets before they sold them to the Indians.

John Slocum looked up that trader, but was too late. The Sioux did it for him at the Little Bighorn.

After that time, John Slocum figured his road was cut out for him. Some men would have the comforts of a home and family. John Slocum would know the warmth of camp fires deep in hostile Indian country, the pleasure of icy winter trails with the snow crusting the edge of his Stetson and the handkerchief he kept wrapped around his face to avoid the frostbite. John Slocum would know the barrooms and back rooms of the west—the good men, the mean men, the great men, the small.

He'd shot a few more men since the War. A few more than he could remember, though he dreamed about them sometimes.

And he was calmer about his imminent demise than many another might have been because he'd had more than his share of luck and he figured his time had run out. He'd planted other men. It was his turn now.

He crossed his feet. The preacher was still at the window. The man had big hands, hands that nearly concealed the testament he had clasped behind his back.

Slocum had seen enough death to know that it rarely gave a man much chance for dignity. Hell, on trail drives he had gathered the scraps of good men who'd camped right in the path of a ten-thousand-animal stampede. He'd seen men's parts blown up and hanging from trees. He didn't expect the grim reaper to be logical or kind, and sometimes he suspected that the old boy with the scythe had a strange sense of humor.

The really funny thing was that the whore hadn't even known the damn kid. The Wichita Kid. Now how was that for a name?

John Slocum had been hunting buffalo for the railroad. The railroad had a thousand workers in Gull and every one of them liked to eat three squares, so John Slocum brought in a great wagon load of buffalo hams and humps and tongues. There were fewer buffalo nowadays than there used to be, but on this trip Slocum had found a small herd grazing in a little hollow beside the Milk and set up his tripod and the big old Sharps. He'd killed him three fat cows and the he-daddy of the herd, who'd make mighty tough eating, but maybe the workers could stew him.

One day's hunting, one day's travel back to Gull, and thirty-four dollars in his pocket. John Slocum was feeling restless. He always got that feeling in the fall, just before the snow blew. Maybe it was time for him to ride south, maybe go for gold in the Sierras. He hadn't been in that part of the country since the Lincoln County Wars, when he rode with Billy Bonney's bunch.

One double eagle, two half eagles, four cartwheels, and four bits in his pocket. He used two bits for a hot bath in the back room of the barbershop, another two bits to get himself shaved and slicked down. He waved away the brilliantine, saying, "Naw, I don't want any of that stuff. I don't want to confuse which of us is the whore."

Saturday night in Gull, the men thronging the

streets had plenty of choices. They could gamble in honest games or dishonest games. Strangely, many of them seemed quite indifferent about the honesty. They could drink, they could fight with pistols, knives, or fists—in order of diminishing status—or they could go to the whorehouses which lined the street out of town. Some of them were no more than tents, some were Conestogas, and some were shacks. Two of them, the Blue Lantern and the Abilene House, were genuine go-to-hell two-story houses with painted shutters and real chandeliers in the parlor.

Slocum elbowed his way through the railroad workers who thronged the wooden sidewalks. There were squareheads, micks, chinks, greenhorns, ex-rebs like Slocum, and men who'd ridden with Grant.

Slocum found himself a chair in the back room of an honest gambling joint and played for an hour or so, losing and winning evenly. Bad hands were interesting, good hands were interesting. Slocum hated to play the in-between hands. The players were tight fisted, making four-bit bets when later in the evening they'd be throwing around cartwheels or gold pieces. Slocum pushed back his chair and rose three dollars richer for his hour of play, and even that little winning brought scowls from the too-careful players gathered that night.

John Slocum had ridden into Gull three weeks earlier. He meant to ride out the day after the next. He knew the best two places to eat in town, The Drover's Hotel and Mrs. Sunderland's; the only honest gambling house in town, Tucker's; and the whorehouses. He didn't know a single soul in Gull, and he didn't want to.

He felt curiously detached. It was the effect of too

many people too close. He had had enough of crowds in the War. It was time for him to clear out, head south.

Saturday night was the worst time to visit a whorehouse, but Slocum felt the old urge. It was seven o'clock. At the Abilene, maybe he'd have a little space to himself.

It occurred to him to wonder why he'd take a woman other men would lie with, but he put that down as an inconvenience of his life. If you don't set down roots you can't make many demands.

The girl was named Lena. She wasn't terribly pretty, because she was a whore, and whores were never terribly pretty. They were desirable, and Lena was. She was fairly young, though the Abilene House had many younger girls in its stable, and she had the pale ash-blonde hair of her Scandinavian ancestry. John Slocum stood in the parlor with a glass of pretty good bourbon in his hand. He never took his hat off, because this wasn't that sort of parlor. One cowboy sprawled in a love seat, nearly too drunk to care about the girl who was sitting on his lap. She was whispering in his ear, trying to get him to go upstairs with her. "Oh come on, honey," she whined.

Two girls flanked one of the town merchants. Slocum had seen him at the feed store. He had his hand under one skirt.

Lena stepped into the room seeking a partner. Black mesh stockings disappeared under her short skirt, and her red blouse was open almost to the navel. She concealed only her merchandise. She had pale blue eyes and her eyelashes were as white as her long hair. "I am Lena, yes?" she said to John Slocum.

"I'll just bet you are."

She pouted. "Do you find me—good-looking?"

"Sure I do."

"Then you will go upstairs with me."

He would, and did, following her rump up those narrow stairs past the closed doors that lined both sides of the passageway, smelling men's cigars, women's perfumes, and sex. He was already hard when she opened the door to her crib.

A pallet on a short wooden bed. The whore's pitcher and bowl. A broken-legged oak dresser with its mirror tilted toward the bed. A wooden footstool that looked suspiciously like the milking stool Slocum had used as a kid.

She undid her blouse quickly. "Do you like, mister?"

Her breasts were rather small, with nipples that elongated as long as the joint of his little finger. He cupped one breast and the nipple was hard against the palm of his hand.

"I always like," he muttered as he kissed her.

Her hands were at his crotch, holding him. "Oh!" she said, surprised.

He backed up to lean against the dresser.

Her little face got very serious. "With such a one as you, I must take much time," she said. "I do not wish to hurt myself."

"Hurtin' you was the last thing on my mind." John Slocum pulled off his plainsman's boots and unbuckled his gun belt. He wore the Colt Navy in the cross-draw holster. The cross-draw wasn't as quick as the gunfighter's rig, but it was quick enough, and he could wear it on horseback.

Slocum folded the belt around his holster and set

the gun butt right on the far side of the pallet where he could get at it. If Lena was surprised, she didn't show it. Men were strange.

The dusting between her legs was the same ash blonde, which surprised him some.

He laid his own clothes neatly on the dresser while she lay on the bed fingering herself to make room. Her smell was sweet sap, and he was so hard it hurt.

When he came into her, she was ready, all warm and clutching. He held back at first, letting himself in slow and easy, giving her plenty of time to adjust. Even so, he found himself in depths few had ever visited, and her muscles were quite tight. He lay in her, soaking it up.

His quiet provoked her and her own motions excited her. Soon her hips were bucking under his and her belly was rippling and her careful makeup was running down her cheeks with her sweat and she was saying something in Norwegian, or maybe Swedish—a prayer or a curse, Slocum didn't know which.

After he pulled out of her, they lay in each other's arms until the intimacy embarrassed them and they dressed briskly, friendlier now that business was over.

Slocum could have gone again but he didn't really want to. He'd come as close to her as he meant to.

Downstairs he bought her a drink and took one himself, though he didn't want it. Manners dictated he drink at least one before he hit the street, though he didn't really have an awful lot to say to this girl.

She took the drink and drank it down with the same no-nonsense manner that had characterized her in bed. She was already looking around for another customer.

She found one, a kid not much older than she was. The kid was dressed in a white buckskin jacket with fringes everywhere. His ten-gallon hat soared so high it dwarfed his forehead, and his tiny riding boots must have pinched his toes.

He would have been funny, but there was nothing funny about the two Remington Army revolvers he carried. Gunfighter's rig on the left and right too. He was glowering at Slocum.

Well, men were strange. John Slocum tossed back his drink, touched his Stetson, and said goodbye.

Three hours later John Slocum was at the poker table when the kid caught up to him.

He marched right up to the table, stopped dead, and fixed all his attention on John Slocum, who didn't want or need it. He'd been having a mild run of good luck and the stack of money before him held better than three hundred dollars, which would get him south for the winter in style.

"I'm the Wichita Kid," the kid announced.

"Do tell."

"I'm twenty years old and I've killed me as many men as I have years, and that's white men, not Mexicans or niggers or Indians."

Slocum folded. He couldn't beat a king-high. Easily he slid his chair back so he wouldn't bump into the table coming up. The Wichita Kid was mad. Whether he was dangerous remained to be seen.

"I'm John Slocum," Slocum said.

The kid nodded, too broadly, the way an idiot nods. Close up, John Slocum could see that his gunfighter's rig was spotlessly new. The ivory-handled pistols gleamed.

"I come to call you out," the Wichita Kid said. His hands curved over his holsters like talons.

Well, that cleared the decks. Men dropped out of the game. The joint was packed wall to wall on a Saturday night and everybody plastered themselves against the walls or made themselves scarce, because in a gunfight there's no telling where the bullets would go.

The bartenders dropped behind the bar. A path opened up behind Slocum and the kid.

John Slocum stood, his thumb hooked in the front of his belt. "Why, sure," he drawled. "I never refused an invitation for a dance in my life, but I wouldn't mind knowin' why. Can't be my good looks."

"You was with my woman!"

Surprised, John Slocum rejected the obvious, but the blank in his memory circled him right back to the obvious every time. "You mean Lena?" he asked.

The kid nodded furiously.

Slocum took his gaze off the kid. He also let his right hand hang free beside the butt of his Colt. "Is there anybody in here kin to this boy?" he asked. "Anybody responsible for him? In a minute things will have gone too far, but right now, if anybody cares, they can save his life. I got no grudge against him and I believe he's a little simple in the head. So if anybody knows him or wants to save his life, now's the time."

A couple more men took advantage of the delay to slip out the batwing doors. Somebody else took advantage of the bartender's absence to snatch three or four free drinks from the bottle on the bar. A couple leaned a little closer so they could see everything. Nobody wanted to interfere.

Slocum decided to reason with the kid. "Look, kid," he said, "I don't know if Lena has told you, but she has an awful secret."

The kid's eyes got puzzled but his hands didn't relax. "Secret?"

"Yeah, kid. You see, Lena goes with any man who's got her price. If any man has got five silver dollars or a half eagle, he can lie down with Lena. She don't mind. She likes the work. I hate to be the one to break it to you, but your Lena's a whore."

"You callin' my girl a whore?" The kid's eyes blazed.

"You bet I am. Lena's . . ."

The time for words had ended. Slocum saw in the kid's eyes the flicker of decision. John Slocum wasn't the fastest man in the West, but he wasn't a slow-poke either, and he meant to jerk iron and lay his gun barrel beside the kid's skull, cold-cocking him before he could do damage.

But the kid was too fast for that play, and nearly cost John Slocum his life. He'd judged the kid's speed from his ridiculous rig and his new pistols. He figured that no half-wit could be quick with a pistol. That prejudice nearly did him in. He had his Navy en route to the Wichita Kid's skull when the boy's right-hand pistol spoke, and if Slocum hadn't been half turned to deliver a blow, that slug would have made chitlings of his innards. As it was, the bullet burned along his side and the blow he'd meant smacked the kid in the jaw instead of the temple. As he rocked with the punch that other Remington was

going to talk, and John Slocum gave up every
kind intention he had and loosed one from six
inches to the kid's head. The bullet so shocked him
that he stuck out the tip of his tongue, his eyes
bulged, his hair fluffed, he lost his sombrero, and he
had no more idea of pulling his second trigger than
any other dead man.

The kid crashed into the bar. His first bullet hadn't
done any damage except to Slocum's shirt, and
Slocum's bullet hadn't done any damage except to
the Wichita Kid, so John Slocum figured that would
be an end to it.

Before they dragged the corpse out to the under-
taker's wagon, three special deputies had John Slocum surrounded. All three carried short-barreled ten-
gauge Greeners, in case Slocum was of a mind to
resist. Which he wasn't.

They had him shucked of his gun and locked in
the jail cell so fast it made his head swim. And the
next morning they had the trial. No jury, just a
judge.

John Slocum figured he'd ride right out of town
after the trial. He was using his own name and since
there were probably still some old warrants out on
him, there was no telling what kind of turn things
could take.

But the law, in the person of a stern old judge,
had other plans. "Hanged by the neck until dead."

Slocum's jaw dropped. "If I hadn't popped a cap
on that no-account, he was going to kill me," Slocum protested.

"Case closed," the judge said.

Slocum had been in jail ever since. He wondered
if that was how they got their entertainment here in

Gull, by hanging whoever they could. He'd heard of men being hanged for self-defense in other towns in the West, but that was where the deceased was an important or popular citizen, and the Wichita Kid had gone to his grave unmourned—just another drifter who showed up in town, picked a fight with the wrong man, and got planted.

At first Slocum had been outraged. Nobody listened to his complaints. Then he became philosophical. Times when he should have been hanged, he'd gone free. So maybe this made up for all of those times.

Maybe he should be a little kinder to this preacher. Except for him, he'd had no visitors. Lena, grieving so publicly outside, hadn't visited him. Her mourning was to enrich her daily take. Everybody knew that the newly widowed charged a little more, and Lena could count herself doubly bereaved. Although, strangely enough, she hadn't known the Wichita Kid any better than Slocum. He'd screwed her that afternoon, paid his money, and left. She swore on her mother's Bible that was the only time she had ever seen him. She invented a romance between herself and John Slocum because he, at least, was good in bed. But the kid—"He was nothing special to me," she shrugged.

"What time you got?" Slocum asked the preacher.

"Twenty minutes. Would you like to pray with me?"

"I'd love to pray with you, except for one problem."

"What's that?"

"My knees can't bend. It's an old family failing."

"You can joke at a time like this?"

Slocum felt like asking, "What better time?" but

contented himself with a shrug. He said, "I heard the condemned man always got a good last meal. Fine tradition, preacher. This morning they brought me son-of-a-bitch stew and biscuits, same as every other meal."

Earnestly the preacher said, "Well, they haven't hanged many people in Gull before. You're the very first."

"I'd just as soon they used somebody else for their practice."

The preacher faced the sounds in the outer office. He opened his Bible and began reading from the Twenty-third Psalm—nothing distinct, just a low mumble. He'd sat up late the night before, planning his choices for the condemned man's last walk. He planned to begin with the familiar psalm and move onto some unfamiliar selections in Proverbs and Isaiah—selections which might make the condemned man repent—and then conclude with the parable of the two thieves, intoning, "For today ye shall be with me in Paradise," as the trap fell.

Four men accompanied the turnkey. To his surprise, Slocum knew one of them very slightly. Was it Tombstone? Waco? It would come to him in a moment. Come to think of it, maybe it would never come to him.

"Hello, Jake. Where the hell did we meet before? I know it was somewhere rough, but can't remember just where it was."

The turnkey said, "Come on, preacher. These gents got private business with the prisoner."

Jake was a slight man in his forties with more hair in his chin whiskers and sideburns than on the top of his head. He wore a suit and vest and carried a small gray bowler in his hand.

Jake looked hurt. "Adobe Wells," he said shortly.

"Oh, yes." Now that had been a memorable fight. It was strange that he should forget it. There was Bill Tighlman and one of the Earp brothers, Morgan Earp, and Bat Masterson and himself and Jake. Jake had been a stage driver. Surrounded for five days by Roman Nose and his damn warriors until Bill Tighlman cracked off a shot at the great chief himself, posturing on a ridgetop they later stepped off at a full honest-to-god mile away. One shot, one honest Injun. That's how Tighlman told it afterwards. Slocum never did care for the man, but he was a hell of a rifle shot. And old Jake had been with them through all of it.

"I'm sorry to see you fallen so low, John," Jake said.

"Well, I'll be up again directly," Slocum said. If there was one thing that pained him it was a lugubrious expression.

One of Jake's companions was a tall gent. You could have laid a seamstress's yardstick along his spine and not shown air. "I am Captain Newell," he said. He didn't stick out his hand to shake.

"Morning, Cap'n," Slocum drawled. "You're out of uniform."

The captain was in his middle thirties, dressed the way a gent dresses when he expects to spend a lot of time outdoors. Lightweight tweed jacket and trousers, shoes instead of boots. Slocum could see the bulge of his shoulder holster, and a sort of wild hope charged through his frame. He swung his feet over and sat up. If he could get to that holster, today's events just might have an unforeseen conclusion.

"I'm not in the army," Captain Newell said. "It's an honorary title from the War."

"I see. I'm Captain Slocum, C. S. A."

"Take it easy, John," Jake said. "We're here to help you."

Slocum's eyes glittered. He stood up. He wasn't so very far from the Yank's pistol holster, and time was short.

The third man in the party wasn't much to look at. He wasn't much bigger than a girl, and he dressed like a dude. His foulard matched his jacket and his pants, and his shoes were glossy cordovan. The cane he held in his right hand had a gold ferrule in the figure of a gooseneck. He said, "Stand back, Captain; I believe the prisoner has intentions on your revolver."

When John Slocum looked at the dude, the dude had a .41 over-and-under derringer leveled at his midsection. Now, that .41 won't do much damage over twenty-five feet and the recoil was terrific, but up close it was a sure ticket on the last express.

The captain stepped back, startled.

Slocum grinned. He flexed his long supple fingers.

"Name's Selkirk," the little man said, introducing himself. "Jay Nelsh's personal secretary."

"If Mr. Nelsh wants something from me, he better get it fast. Another fifteen minutes and I'm gonna be gone," Slocum said.

Jay Nelsh—dreamer, engineer, financier. Slocum had never met the man, though he'd seen him several times en route between the railhead back in Fargo and end of track somewhere in the badlands. Rumor said Nelsh was out here to hurry construction.

He had eighty more miles of track to lay before snow came. Others said he was out here because his creditors were back East, at the far end of his railroad track. Slocum didn't know which story to believe.

"What do you know about Mr. Nelsh?" the dude asked.

Slocum's jaw set. "Friend, we haven't much time to continue this conversation on this earthly plane. If you got something to say, I suggest you spit it out."

The dude laughed, a couple of honking snorts. "You are quick, aren't you, Mr. Slocum?"

"Yeah. That's why I'm here."

Captain Newell cleared his throat. He extracted a piece of paper from his waistcoat. It looked like a letter folded three times. "I have here a pardon for you, signed by the Territorial Governor."

Slocum whooshed the air between his teeth. He pulled out his little bag of Bull Durham and carefully rolled himself a quirly. When he was done, he inquired quietly, "Don't suppose you'd have a match, too?"

The captain went red in the face. "I have here a pardon. It's valid. Good as gold."

He waved it in Slocum's face, but Slocum cupped his hands to get a light from Nelsh's secretary. "Who is Captain Newell, Jake?" Slocum asked.

Jake got all awkward. Slocum had enlisted him under his own banner, and Jake wasn't so sure that was wise. "He's Jay Nelsh's detective, Mr. Slocum. The head detective."

"You mean he's head of Nelsh's thugs?"

Captain Newell snapped, "We guard railroad property and protect Mr. Nelsh himself."

Slocum laughed. "Yeah, that's what I meant. Railroad thugs."

"I don't like your attitude, Slocum."

"So hang me."

"I'm here to offer you a chance to save your life, and you mock me. I have half a mind to rescind my offer."

Once again, John Slocum shrugged. "Got a hunch there's a price tag on your help."

Captain Newell sneered, "Unknown drifter like you? What do you have that I want?"

John Slocum spent a few seconds memorizing the captain's face so he'd know him the next time he ran across him. He had too young a face on a middle-aged body. His hair was carefully slicked back and not a single hair was out of place.

Apparently, the wordless scrutiny irritated the captain because, against his will, he took a step backward.

The little dude spoke. "We're here to offer you work," he said.

Slocum spoke very quietly. "I don't suppose it might be gun work?"

The dude's eyebrows climbed up on his forehead. "Is there some other kind of work you do?"

It was Slocum's turn to be taken aback. Mentally he started listing the other jobs he could do: there was bronc buster and trail boss; he'd slaughtered beeves and skinned them. He'd hunted buffalo and he'd hunted men. He grinned. "Yeah. I see what you mean."

Quite pleasantly, Captain Newell said, "All you rebel scum will kill for hire."

Slocum already had Newell marked and, since he was talking to a dead man, he didn't reply.

Jake said, "Jesus, John, don't be like that. We're here to save your damn worthless hide." Jake added, "Ha, ha." Nobody else saw anything funny.

"What's the job?" Slocum asked.

"Mr. Nelsh needs a bodyguard," the dude explained pleasantly.

Slocum jerked a thumb. "You mean the cap'n here can't handle the job?"

Captain Newell said, "I can assure you, Slocum, my recommendation—"

"I'll just bet it was," Slocum interrupted. "So you've got a pardon for me if I get between Mr. Nelsh and whoever wants to kill him. Who might that be?"

"I'm not at liberty to tell," the captain said.

John Slocum sat down again and swung his feet back onto the bunk. He tipped his hat over his eyes. "I'd like to get a little shut-eye," he said. "When I dance at the end of the rope, I don't want to quit before the music does."

"What?" The captain was flabbergasted.

Slocum closed his eyes, but his ears were extremely keen.

"You reject our pardon?"

Slocum tipped his hat back. "There's worse things than hanging, you know," he said. "One of them is getting set up for a hanging. Now, Jake, I want you to come over here and look me right in the eye."

Jake shambled near, twisting his bowler in his hand. "What do you want? I don't know . . ."

Slocum fixed his yellow eyes on Jake's soft brown ones. He meant to have the truth, even if it was by main force. "Jake, I want you to think all the way back to Adobe Wells. I want you to remember that first morning when you went out to feed the horses, not knowing there was a redskin in a hundred miles. And there they were, and you had no way of getting back to the blockhouse unless somebody came out and drew their fire while you ran. Ain't that so, Jake?"

The man nodded. He wetted his lips.

"You're in my debt, Jake."

"I reckon I am."

"You ever see the Wichita Kid before?"

Jake shot a desperate glance at Jay Nelsh's secretary and chief of security. They wouldn't meet his gaze.

Slocum bored on. "That crazy half-wit, Kid Wichita—one of you bastards hired him, didn't you?"

Jake licked his lips. Defiantly, he said, "I ain't sayin' whether it's so or it isn't."

"Oh, Jesus Christ," Slocum said. "You sent him after me, pumped him up with what a great damn gunfighter he was, and when I dropped him, you and your pet judge sentenced me to hang. What a fine bunch of vultures you are."

"We felt you wouldn't wish to undertake the job under other circumstances," the captain said swiftly.

"You were right enough there."

For a second time the keys jangled. The turnkey and the preacher returned. It may have been his imagination, but John Slocum swore the crowd noise had grown. They were smelling his death.

As soon as the preacher saw John Slocum he started up on the Twenty-third Psalm again. If he rushed, he might get through all his planned selections before Slocum took the drop.

". . . leadeth me beside the still waters . . ."

Captain Newell held the paper up. "Well, what do you say?"

". . . restoreth my soul. Yea, though I walk through the valley of the shadow of death . . ."

"Jake," Slocum sighed, "you disappoint me." But he took the pardon and the job.

3

It was a big crowd, and it had come a long way.
There weren't very many social events in the Dakotas,
and fewer still on the edge of the badlands. Since
there weren't any churches, no church socials; no
fraternal organizations meant no dances on Saturday
nights. Nobody had lived here long enough to de-
velop comfortable family reunions and without any
schools, school reunions were out. Births, funerals,
weddings, and hangings pretty much made up the
list of social gatherings—and the first three were
really family affairs.

Hangings were everyone invited and come as you
are.

Nesters had brought their wives and kids and de-
posited the wives at Arnie Nelson's Mercantile with
the kids in tow so they could eyeball cloth from the
great heavy bolts of gingham and calico while their
brood sucked on penny candy.

Cowhands gathered at the Silver Dollar Saloon
where they spoke of stampedes and the newfangled
barbed-wire fence and the pros and cons of the
big Herefords some outfits were bringing in from
Oregon.

The gaming tables weren't doing very much
business. Oddly enough—and every tinhorn West of
the Mississippi knew it—nothing cooled a man's
gambling urges more than a gunfight or a hanging.
Tinhorns just folded up for the morning and sought

good places to watch the scheduled execution from the boardwalk outside.

Hotel rooms facing the gallows were available for fifty dollars gold, one hundred times the normal rate. The two hotel balconies were crowded with chairs and the chairs rented for this occasion at five dollars each.

One Eastern sport rented a suite of rooms with six windows overlooking the gallows, ordered cases of champagne and boxes of cigars, and invited all his friends to the gala. The cigar smoke inside the room was so thick they had all the windows open and, to those unfortunates who hadn't been invited, the smoke billowing out of those windows made it seem as if the damn hotel was on fire.

Respectable women watched from the hotel balconies or took folding chairs to the roof of Nelson's Mercantile across the street. The soiled doves parked their surrey right in the middle of the street, and Lena was a most important celebrity.

The Alamo Saloon had a barrel of whiskey set up outside its front doors and two bartenders sweated, keeping up with the crowd. Hawkers and pickpockets slipped through the crowd, working their special skills.

The low-class whores waited in the alleys and more than one man relieved his tension with them, shoving against the back wall of Lawson's Feeds or the National Bank of Gull.

Two special deputies guarded the gallows itself, or people would have taken seats on the wooden planks just to get closer. Already kids had whittled chunks out of the wooden supports for souvenirs. By

the end of the day, the damn thing would look like
woodpeckers had been at it.

The hangman had been brought in special from St.
Paul. A jolly, sweating, fat-faced man, he'd only
arrived the day before with his trunks of flamboyant
checked suits and fancy, floppy ties. He also had a
very small bag which held his coiled rope. After the
hanging, as was his custom, he'd sell off hanks of
rope, six inches long, at fifty cents each. It was a
good price for a rope he'd never trust again anyway.
Hanging a man took all the life out of a rope.

He'd tested the trap and the weights and found
them satisfactory. He'd eyeballed John Slocum and
estimated his height—six foot, one inch—and weight—
190. He wasn't off by much. He never was. He'd
want the drop to break Slocum's neck, not tear his
head off or strangle him slowly. A row of six chairs
waited behind the hangman as he made fussy little
final adjustments to the rope. His hood drooped out
of the pocket of his dark blue suit. He hated to put
the hot thing on until the prisoner was led out of the
jail.

The chairs were for dignitaries. The judge, the
sheriff, a journalist from the Minneapolis *Star* who'd
traveled all the way out here for the story.

A photographer set up his heavy camera on the far
corner of the platform. When the execution was
ready, just in the moment before the trap fell, he'd
release his flash powder and press the shutter. If he
caught it just right, he'd have a picture of John
Slocum's last moment of life. If he was premature,
Slocum might twitch or move and if he shot an
instant too late, all he'd capture would be a streak on
his plate.

At most hangings the guest of honor was pretty well known. Usually there was a big family to grieve and carry on. Usually the man he killed had family too, waiting to see justice done. The two families often found themselves sitting close together, directly in front of the gallows, and students of human nature liked to get as near as they could to overhear any interchanges between them. But in this case there were no families and apparently no friends. The Wichita Kid was a total unknown. He might as well have dropped into Gull from the moon. Nobody claimed to have known him before. Rumors were quite fantastic. The Wichita Kid, it was said, had ridden with Jesse James, Cole Younger, the Daltons, the Earps, Doc Holliday, Sam Bass, take your pick. He was said to be a Pinkerton, a railroad thug, and a fully ordained minister of the Gospel.

The stories were so contradictory that the reporter for the Minneapolis *Star* had it in his notes that he was "another high-plains drifter, come to a sorry end in a barroom fight."

John Slocum was better known. A man by the name of Frank Bahnson had ridden with him when he ramrodded trail herds north out of Texas just after the war. Bahnson was quite happy to recount his tales of the days on the trail with Slocum to anyone who had the price of a drink. "He was a hard man, but he was fair." Bahnson shook his finger at his listeners. "And there wasn't a better man to have at your side when the Comanches came after you or the herd was spooky. I never knew John Slocum to do a dishonorable thing," said the town drunk.

Another man, a guest of the rich man in the champagne hotel room, had known John Slocum during the War when, as he put it, "Slocum was just a snot-nosed kid, green as grass, but a hell of a hand with any kind of rifle. I believe that kid accounted for as many blue-bellies as any of us. Never bragged about it either. Always was a quiet one." The man checked his repeater. "They're a little late, aren't they? I've got ten past, and they haven't brought him out of the jailhouse yet."

The dignitaries had all arrived, except for the sheriff, who was inside with the prisoner. The crowd at the foot of the gallows was a solid wall, so dense that the pickpockets couldn't get into the pockets they saw. The crowd was getting sullen as the minutes dragged on.

"Where is he?"

"I don't know."

"Where is he?"

"I told you, I don't know. If I knew, I would have said so, wouldn't I? Take your elbow out of my side, you son of a bitch."

With a bang the jailhouse door opened and the sheriff hurried toward the platform. Everybody's hopes picked up again. Slowly the sheriff pushed through the crowd. He was holding a document above his head.

The executioner slipped on his black mask and faced the jailhouse door.

The sheriff stepped to the front of the platform and held up both hands for silence.

"I got an announcement. Important announcement. Ladies and gents, be quiet now so you can all hear the announcement." When he had his silence, he plucked his spectacles from his breast pocket and read: "By the authority vested in me as Governor of

Dakota Territory, I hereby pardon John Slocum of the murder of the person known as the Wichita Kid, signed under my hand, this year of our Lord, September fifth, 1881.''

The sheriff returned his glasses to their case and folded the pardon. The judge got to his feet and demanded to see the document. The crowd groaned and howled.

The executioner practically tore the hood off his head. His face was apple-skin red, and sweat made it shiny. He thought about the fee he wouldn't collect, the rope hanks nobody would want.

Someone in the crowd stated what was on everybody's mind. "I didn't ride three days from the North Fork of the Yellowstone for this!"

The hangman lifted his face to the uncaring sky and cried, "It ain't fair! It just isn't justice!"

The crowd roiled and curled, like a snake somebody had stepped on. Its brains and its eyes were everywhere. A voice called out, "They're takin' him out the back of the jail!"

And the crowd put on its purpose, funneling toward the far side of the jail, men running, women and children getting out of the way. The bawds from the Abilene House whipped their surrey into hot pursuit and two Morgans plunged forward, oblivious of the damage they would cause.

Jake, Slocum, Captain Newell, and the little secretary were in Jay Nelsh's coach, pulled by four fine horses. The best coach you could rent in Gull and the best rented horses, too. When the fastest part of the crowd rounded the jail, they saw the back of that coach just turning down the long hill that led to the river and Jay Nelsh's railroad.

"They're running for the train!"

It wasn't clear what the crowd had on its mind. Some of the pursuers undoubtedly wanted to see Slocum, or somebody, hang. Some of the pursuers chased just because the quarry fled. Some went along for the sport. They pelted along as fast as they could run behind the coach, and the sound of their passage was like white water crashing. They followed the racing coach, running downhill, and some fell when their bodies outran their legs. These limped along when they got up and cursed their torn and dirty clothes. The whorehouse surrey broke past the leaders and gained on the coach. The women's scarves fluttered behind them like gay pennants in the wind.

Waiting at the bottom of the hill was a long transcontinental locomotive of the newest design, polished, all black and nickel and brass. It was chuffing, and the smoke from the funnel was an uninterrupted flow. Behind the locomotive the tender was just as black as the engine and topped off with the hottest-burning anthracite coal. Engine and tender were strong, powerful machines, and the private car they drew was of the same breed. It was a deep, deep navy blue, almost blue-black, just slightly lighter than the bluing on a Colt's revolver. The arabesques around the coach windows were pure gold leaf. The brass rail at the end platform sparkled in the afternoon sun and a black porter was just running a final rag over the rail, ignoring the howling mob.

Between the fleeing party and the train lay Gull's pride and joy, the new stockyards. They were like an obstacle course. Slocum and the others hurried over the first of those corrals and became completely undignified in doing so. A man could flee with dignity in a coach. A man clambering over a fence looked ridiculous. The black man unlatched the little brass gate and stood politely as the men puffed toward him. He put on his porter's smile.

The engineer put the steam to the driving wheels and the locomotive jerked into motion. As the three men scrambled over the last obstacle, the train was already picking up speed and drawing away from them.

Inside, the young woman heard the noise, of course, but she didn't bother to lift the lace curtain that screened her breakfast table from the outside world. She'd heard noises outside her daddy's private train before—that time in Chicago when the strikers rioted and some of them actually reached Nelsh's private car before being shot off the rear platform by his guards. She had hated it. The car had been just full of guards, as crowded as a regular railroad coach with armed, sweating men. The air had reeked of liquor fumes, tobacco smoke, and the stink of fear. The strangers quite took over, seated at the dining-room table, sprawled on the couches in the parlor area. Elizabeth Nelsh had retired to her own tiny bedroom and locked the door. She didn't pull the curtains aside, even when she heard the actual sound of a bullet thumping into a wall of the car and the moans of the wounded. One man fell below her window. He slid along the car from the back to the front. She could hear his jacket against the metal and even the tiny clicks of his buttons, scratching the deep blue paint. He grunted, too, like a little pug dog she had had as a child, pushing his hurt body along. She could trace his progress exactly from one side of her bedroom to the other. She was afraid and she didn't open the drapes.

Why should she be curious now? No shots, just shouts. Her daddy was in front of the car with his engineer. He wouldn't notice either. He never did. She could hear the murmur of their discussion, the engineer's tones and her father's shrill ones.

The car carried four black male servants. One of them hovered near her table right now and when the locomotive threw its wheels into its work, his dark hand flashed out to keep her silver teapot from sliding into her lap. " 'Scuse me, Missy," he said, smiling. "I wouldn't want you burnin' yourself."

"Thank you. You can take it away. We seem to be moving, and I loathe tepid tea."

The servant wasn't quite as sanguine as his mistress. Mr. Nelsh's trains got into the damnedest spots sometimes.

He turned his head when he heard the unmistakable clump of feet on the rear platform. Two servants waited with silver-handled whisk brushes.

There was a shout of rage. The crowd howled like maddened animals as their quarry began to draw away.

The back of the car, where the four men entered, had a narrow door with "N" set right in the middle of the etched glass. This couldn't usually be seen from inside the car because the curtain of wine-red cut velvet was almost always drawn. Mr. Nelsh liked the car dark, and his daughter hadn't ever known it any other way.

Within ornate gold frames flanking the door were two small Flemish paintings, a picture of a smiling, gap-toothed boy and a study of skaters on the Zuider Zee.

The private car boasted a fireplace complete with carved walnut mantel. Above the mantel was a Stubbs watercolor of Nelsh's famous racehorse: Northern Lights. The furniture in the car was all heavy walnut or cherry. A heavy library table held Lizzie Nelsh's modest breakfast of eggs, smoked salmon, tea biscuits, and a rosette of creamery butter on a tiny silver tray. She sat on the straight-backed brocaded chair with one leg curled up under her. She was a little thing, not more than five feet four inches, and the furniture had been designed for barons and earls.

Lizzie had been Jay Nelsh's companion since her mother's death fifteen years before. Now she was engaged to Captain Newell, a match her father didn't approve of but didn't forbid either. She hoped her father wanted her to follow the dictates of her heart. She feared he didn't care.

Jay Nelsh was tall and reed-slender, with the appetite of a baby sparrow and the physique of an underfed chimpanzee. The servants cut his lanky black hair when it started getting in his eyes. Her father loved to read from Ruskin, William Morris, and the poet Browning. When Dickens had made his lecture tour to America, Nelsh had sought him out and talked with the famous man for nearly three hours— about ideas, of course.

Captain Newell, Lizzie thought, was everything her father could never be. Bold and adventurous, a man of hot blood and energy.

She put her feet down on the thick carpet and announced that she was quite finished. Just then the

back door burst open and four animals—no, men—
were there, sucking air into their lungs and leaning
against the bulkhead.

"Watch out for those pictures," Lizzie called out
sharply. One of the men, Selkirk, her father's personal secretary, ushered the others away from danger.
The locomotive engineer had the throttle wide open
now.

Lizzie saw Selkirk, Captain Newell, Jake—the
Captain's dogsbody—and a stranger. She couldn't
take her eyes off that stranger.

"Christ," Jake said, "that was close. Pardon or
no pardon, they were ready to string somebody up."

"Watch your language, man!" Selkirk snapped.

Jake removed his Stetson and apologized through
his gasps.

The stranger had green eyes just like the stones on
the brooch her daddy had given her the previous
Christmas.

The stranger grinned at her and, deliberately,
winked.

"Oh!" Lizzie said, putting a hand to her mouth.

"Sorry, Miss Nelsh," the captain said formally.
"We didn't mean to frighten you like this, but it was
getting a little hot back there."

Lizzie could still hear shouts, though they were
much fainter.

"Surprised they didn't resort to gunplay," Selkirk
said in that funny, clipped accent of his.

"They didn't want to up the stakes," Slocum
said. "They start, we start, and more'n one man
would die. They were too civilized for gunplay. But
if they'd caught up with us, I would be doin' my
death dance right now."

"You don't seem too disturbed about it."

Slocum shrugged. He walked over to the table. "Coffee in that pot, ma'am?"

"No," Lizzie said, rather startled. She was accustomed to being addressed only by her equals, of which there were few. Captain Newell probably wasn't even her equal. Her daddy said he wasn't. Lizzie didn't care about that as much as her daddy did. The captain was her ticket out of the dark private car and the dark mansion in St. Paul and the discussions she wasn't expected to join, held behind closed doors. Though she hardly knew it, Lizzie sought the fresh air as eagerly as any flower.

"That pot holds tea. It's Ceylonese with orange blossoms. Would you like a cup?"

"That'd be fine."

"Slocum," Newell cautioned, "in Mr. Nelsh's employ, the help don't dine with their betters. Lizzie is Mr. Nelsh's daughter."

"All right," Slocum said affably. "I'll not take any sugar in the tea but I'd take a dollop of that cream, if you would."

"Slocum," Captain Newell warned, "I told you . . ."

"Friend," Slocum drawled, "I have taken bread with Massa Robert—that's General Robert E. Lee to you. I have got drunk several times with James Butler Hickok—a man you might have heard of as Wild Bill. I have smoked with Sitting Bull, Chief of all the Hunkpapa Sioux. I expect it'll be all right if I take a cup of tea with this pretty young lady."

The captain's face went beet-red. "I'll see you later," he said.

Again that infuriating grin. "Any time, any place," Slocum said. He sat down then, right beside Miss

Lizzie Nelsh, and waited for the servant to bring him his cup.

She looked at him and something in her breast squeezed and jumped, as if there was a small animal in there trying to get out.

"Name's Slocum, ma'am. John Slocum. I'll be with you for a spell—seein' you and your daddy come to no harm."

"I can take care of myself," Lizzie retorted.

"Yes, ma'am, I'm sure you can. But I was in a bit of a tight spot back there and I had to promise most anything to get me out, even promising that I'd help protect somebody who didn't need protecting because she was quite capable of taking care of herself. This tea is really something, ma'am. I don't believe I've ever tasted anything quite so good as this tea."

"Slocum," the captain warned.

"Now I've got everybody interested in takin' from your teapot, ma'am."

"Slocum, this has gone far enough!"

Slocum's grin was innocent. "Yes, sir, I expect it has. I expect that somewhere down the track you'll just have to put me off, for my uppity ways. I expect you'll just have to tie the can to my tail, turn me loose, and let me go. I expect you'll have to give me the ax, all right. God, how I'd hate to lose this job!"

"Lizzie," Captain Newell said with steel in his voice, "I want you to return to your bedroom."

Well, think of that! Elizabeth got to her feet, though what was happening was awfully interesting. They were to have a private meeting.

As she passed John Slocum, he whispered to her

just so she could hear, "Takin' care of yourself means makin' up your own mind, Elizabeth."

She turned then, puzzled, and faced all the men. Big Captain Newell was wearing his sternest glower, Selkirk the look of irony he always wore, and John Slocum had a quirky grin pasted on his face like nothing could take it off. She hesitated. It wasn't for long, but it was the first hesitation she'd ever shown obeying a man's orders. She went into her room and leaned against the door, suddenly weary. She went over and knelt on her little bunk bed to hurl her curtains open on the sagebrush, the cracked coulees, the wild things that were out there, all through the world.

"Slocum," Captain Newell said, "we're going to have a little talk."

John Slocum came out of his lazy slouch and faced the bigger man. The grin seemed carved on his face, and it was an infuriating grin.

Jake got between the two men, waving his ineffectual hands. "No sense fighting among ourselves. No sense in that at all."

The secretary, Selkirk, watched them all with a curiously detached smile, like a man watching zoo animals.

"Slocum, Miss Lizzie Nelsh is my fiancée. I'll thank you to not interfere with her."

"A cup of tea?"

"Slocum, you are not of her class. You are beneath her. I do not wish to see you aspire to what you may not achieve."

Slocum never lost that grin. "Funny thing, Newell, I'd guess that Mr. Selkirk here might have some of the breeding you're talking about, but I surely don't see it in you."

They would have gone for it right there if the door to Nelsh's office hadn't opened. Someone popped his head out to say, "You gentlemen may come in now."

The office occupied a quarter of the long railroad car. Surveyors' drawings were pinned to the walls and lay in an unruly stack on the great oak table. The windows were covered with charts of the railroad's progress, graphs which showed the rise and fall of its financial fortunes on Wall Street, alone and compared to other construction railroads and non-construction railroads like the New York Central, whose expenses were exclusively maintenance.

Nelsh was as cadaverous as President Lincoln and his hair was unkempt. Cigar ash stained his shirt and sparks had burned tiny holes here and there. He had the palest blue eyes John Slocum had ever seen, and his wide mouth held the ready smile of a dreamer. When he looked at you with those eyes, there was no telling what he really saw. Some said it was like getting bored with a drill bit. Others claimed he focused somewhere behind their heads and hardly saw them at all. Men often felt the urge to touch him, to make him like the rest of us, and men who were rarely demonstrative or overtly physical found themselves tugging at his sleeve or pushing him so that he must, simply must, examine the newest financial chart, pushing him toward some job of work they wanted him for once to actually see, damn it, not just slide on past like it wasn't there with no more than a faint compliment.

He fixed his eyes on Slocum right from the start. He cocked his head, waiting for explanations.

Selkirk provided them. "This is Mr. Slocum," he drawled. "He's your new bodyguard."

Nelsh's eyes wandered all over John Slocum as though he'd never quite seen the like.

Another man at the long table stood up and pushed his hand at Captain Newell. "Captain, I'm Welfleet, U. S. Senate. I've heard nothing but good things about you. The West could use more men of your stamp."

Welfleet wore a bottle-green suit and a banker's Stetson, which rested beside an ashtray.

The next man to stretch out his hand was a dapper gent with a rather tight gray pinstripe suit and a platinum watch chain. His watch was platinum too, if the case was the same as the stem that peeped so discreetly from his waistcoat pocket. His cuffs were shot back, revealing an expanse of creamy yellow silk and his black onyx studs. His hair was brushed straight back from his forehead and his little moustache held about fourteen hairs to the left of his nostrils and the same number to the right.

The other three men at the table were in shirt-sleeves. They were Nelsh's chief engineers, and they nodded their awkward nods and waited to get back to the real business of building a railroad.

When Nelsh spoke, his voice was remarkably soft, as soft as a whisper. "Have you killed many men?" he asked.

"More'n I ever wished to," Slocum replied. There was something in Nelsh's voice that commanded honesty.

"Has it changed you, do you think?" Nelsh's forehead was furrowed.

There are questions that should not be put. In the West it was considered bad manners to ask about a man's past, his former name, or his antecedents. If a man wanted to reveal such things, he would reveal them without prompting. Until that time, one restrained one's curiosity.

A man didn't ask how it felt to kill another man— not unless he was willing to chance joining the earlier victim. But Nelsh was not an ordinary man— not an ordinary questioner.

"Yes," Slocum said. "It hardens you." He felt strange answering, but he did not regret it.

Nelsh nodded. "Good to have you with us. We'll speak about your duties." He turned his pale gaze on his secretary. "Senator Welfleet believes we won't reach our estimated distance this year before the snow comes. Our stock is endangered and our financiers are quite nervous." When Selkirk opened his mouth, Nelsh went on, "That was not an invitation for your comment, Selkirk, since you are neither a money man nor an engineer. I merely wish to keep you in the picture."

"Sir."

"And, Captain Newell, if Senator Welfleet is correct, there are rumors of some monstrous plot against my life. Your fears were justified, and your intelligence sources are confirmed. There are those who wish to break the railroad and who will murder me to do so. You must not allow that."

He was talking as if the threatened man was not himself. "Nothing must be allowed to delay the railroad," he added.

One of the shirt-sleeved engineers nodded his approval. The other one unfolded a great map and began making more calculations.

"Gentlemen," Nelsh said, "will you excuse me and Mr. Slocum?"

They all filed out of the car except Slocum and the confidential secretary, Selkirk. While Nelsh and Slocum talked, Selkirk emptied the overflowing ashtrays and attempted to restore some order to the big room.

"Let me tell you what's at stake," Nelsh began. "I don't want any men to work for me without knowing the risks. By an act of Congress the railroads are given alternating sections of land, six hundred forty acres in each section along the right-of-way. That land, some of which is the most fertile land in this country, is the guarantee financiers have that the railroad can't fail. In return for that concession, I must reach a certain point in each of four years of construction, the point this year being mile eight hundred thirty. The ground is surveyed and cleared, the grades have been dug, and so long as we lay rail between now and December thirtieth, title for thousands of acres of land will pass into our hands and from us into the hands of settlers who wish to open this vast prairie up for progress."

Slocum's expression was impassive. He wasn't so sure about progress. When he first came out West it wasn't nearly so crowded nor so civilized, and he'd liked it fine.

"Yes, sir. Millions of dollars in land are held in escrow until we complete the last eighty miles of track. The December thirtieth deadline is artificial, of course. We shall go on until the snow gets too deep for work—a date which we estimate as October fifteenth.''

''That's late.''

''You know these plains?''

''I've ridden them a time or two. I've seen three-foot snows in September.''

''I've studied the weather predictions,'' Nelsh said. ''Our estimate is October fifteenth.''

''Have it your way.''

Nelsh's first smile was extraordinarily warm. It was a smile that invited complicity in mischief. ''Mr. Slocum, I generally do.''

Selkirk stacked maps and survey charts, patting their edges to align them.

''I suppose you know that fellow with the senator?'' Slocum asked.

''Yes. He's an important Austrian financier, Count Deleis. If he decides to invest in the railroad, other Europeans will follow, and the difficulty we have with working capital right now will clear up.''

''Count who?''

''Count Deleis. He was introduced to me by Senator Welfleet.''

''Uh-huh.''

Selkirk had stopped his housecleaning and was all ears. The sentences Slocum had meant to speak never left his lips. ''All right,'' he said. ''Fine. Let's get the ground rules straight between us. I'm to protect you and your railroad, is that right?''

''Yes. Your employment was Captain Newell's idea.''

''You know how they did it?'' Slocum asked.

''No, sir. I don't concern myself with details. Get the right man for the job, then let him do it—that's my motto. And those are your ground rules. I don't wish to answer questions from you every day or even every other day. You report to Captain Newell.''

"How long a job?"

"As long as you wish."

"Suppose I don't wish it very long?"

"Then suppose you work for me until the work is stopped this year. Once track reaches mile eight hundred thirty, the real danger should be over."

John Slocum hesitated. He didn't want the job under any conditions. He didn't like the players. Nelsh was all right and his daughter was awfully good-looking, though terribly sheltered. Captain Newell had struck a wrong note from the beginning. If he was any judge, the secretary, Selkirk, had courage but wouldn't be very much help when the bullets flew. He didn't like one inch of Senator Welfleet and he knew Count Deleis under a different name. He'd let that fact rest. For allies he had the people he was supposed to protect and good old Jake, who hadn't been a pillar of strength at Adobe Wells when he was younger and braver.

"I'll want a good bit of pay for this," he said. "A thousand dollars until the snow flies."

"A thousand dollars for two months' work?"

"I figure one month."

"I pay my engineers a hundred dollars a month. My accountant gets seventy-five. Captain Newell gets seventy-five."

"If you ain't alive when I come for my wages I won't take them," Slocum said.

Nelsh laughed. "Put her there," he said, and stuck out his gangly paw. He had a good grip.

Nelsh called for his engineers. If he could put

together a second crew of track layers at the railhead, he could work around the clock. He and his engineers were reworking their rosters—which superintendents would work which shifts, which foremen could handle additional responsibility, which track layers aspired to be foremen.

John Slocum strolled through the car to the little platform. Two tracks wide, side by side, east- and west-bound. When the Union Pacific had completed its track, the passengers could shoot from the windows into vast herds of buffalo. Passengers on the Great Northern some fifteen years later would be lucky if they saw a single animal. The passengers on the first transcontinental trains had dined on breast of passenger pigeon. They had already become scarce. The hunters who'd once brought in thousands brought them in by tens, and nobody was rich enough to eat just the breast meat any more.

Slocum eyed the tall bunch grass—the grass that had tickled the bellies of the first horses to cross the plains early mapmakers named the Great American Desert. Slocum tried to imagine what they would look like when Nelsh had his way and plows turned the black soil to the sun for the first time ever.

He started to work up his Colt. The revolver had lain in the jailhouse at Gull for a full week, and no telling who'd been fooling with it. The Colt Navy was a percussion pistol and Slocum withdrew five number nine percussion caps, one at a time, and pulled the charges, too.

He recharged the cylinders one at a time, checking each conical bullet against the light for scars. Nicked bullets wouldn't fly true. Though there were plenty of cartridge pistols available after the first Colt Army in '73, Slocum and a good many other pistoleros still preferred the old Navy. If you couldn't kill a man with the first five, fast reloading wouldn't save you, and the Navy could get off the all-important first shot faster than any other revolver ever made. The exquisite balance of the Navy Colt made marksmen out of dunderers and gunfighters of beginners. In the hands of men like John Slocum, Bill Hickok, Wesley Hardin, and a handful of others, the Navy would shoot with a rifle to a hundred and fifty yards. Colt sold little shoulder stocks that turned the pistol into a carbine, but Slocum never thought they were any great advantage. The carbine stock never lengthened the seven and a half inches of barrel, and barrel length did affect accuracy. What you set against your shoulder generally didn't. It was an exceptional revolver, and there were any number of better carbines.

The door opened behind him. Miss Nelsh saw the pistol. ''Put that thing away!'' she cried.

He withdrew an oiled cloth from his possibles sack and rubbed the browned frame of the revolver, removing the fingerprints.

''Perhaps you didn't hear me.''

''Yes, ma'am. If you don't keep a light film of oil on your pistol, it'll rust when human fingers touch it. I've seen some thumbprints on pistols that were as clear as the printing on a postage stamp.''

He was particularly scrupulous with his oiling and, in fact, took longer with the job than he needed to.

Her face changed from the imperious to the childlike. ''Mr. Slocum,'' she said, ''why don't you do as I say?''

That earned her a brief grin. "Because what you say ain't right."

"Well, I think pistols are ugly."

"Yes, ma'am."

"They're horrible."

"I should certainly hope so. If what I carried wasn't ugly and horrible, it wouldn't kill the fellows who are fixing to kill your dad. Can't do killing work with a bunch of daisies." Satisfied with his inspection, he holstered the Colt. "This your first trip out West?"

"No, indeed. I've been out West many times with my father. We've been building this railroad for years now, and I travel everywhere with him."

"You ever get out of this fancy car?"

"Why should I?" she asked in genuine puzzlement.

He looked her up and down. She felt weighed in the balance, like gold dust in a pan or rye flour in the grocer's scale. She felt judged. She didn't like it, either—not a bit. "Sir, since you are so very interested in my face and—uh—person, perhaps you will let your views be known."

"You got eyes to see with, a mouth to make your wants known, arms thin as kindling, and breasts and hips that'd raise strong young'uns. You always had everything except what you needed. You dress good. I'll bet that little blue skirt cost a week's wages. But in a big crowd you'd vanish. You don't much want to be a woman—you'd rather be a child."

She didn't know what made her do it. She put her lips on his and, though she'd kissed before, politely with relatives and lady acquaintances, perfunctorily with the boys who'd sought her at dances, and what she thought to be passionately with Captain Newell, on their one night together in that unfortunate hotel on Chicago's Gold Coast, her kiss surprised her. She went straight for it, and never veered. No coyness, no charm, nothing in it to turn her back into herself. Her kiss offered a trade—his soul for hers—and accepted no cheaper substitute. To her further surprise, he returned her kiss, open and seeking like her own.

He was a stranger. They'd just been introduced. She was another man's fiancée. She always lived up to her promises. Captain Newell was going to take her away.

But none of it mattered a bit.

When finally they broke off, she felt a curious languor, as if she'd eaten a bit too much, or the way she felt at the end of a day so lovely she couldn't wish for another hour of it.

"I was wrong about one thing," Slocum said.

He had never taken his eyes off her face all the while. How extraordinary! "What's that?" she asked.

"You ain't no child."

4

Jay Nelsh viewed men as tools, tools more or less useful for building his great railroad. It would be proper to say that he had no attitude toward John Slocum at all. He had consulted with old Jake and Captain Newell, both of whom had particular attitudes about Slocum's reputation and skills. Jake thought Slocum was a man of great integrity; the captain thought Slocum was a hired gun. Nelsh had met John Slocum, read his eyes, and made his choice. If Nelsh was in terrible danger, this Slocum would protect him. When John Wilkes Booth's bullet killed the President fifteen years ago, all men despaired of protecting themselves. But, as far as it could be done, this green-eyed gunman would do it.

Building his railroad was the real problem. Sometimes he envied the men who'd rammed through the Union Pacific. Even the Southern Pacific had a lot of patriotic sentiment working for it. But the Northern was a late railroad and crossed the top of the country, and politically, it was less important. Well, Mr. Jay Nelsh didn't count that an insurmountable obstacle. If there was no constituency for his railroad, he would create one—in this country if possible, in Europe if that failed. He sold his rough prairie as "Finer than Pennsylvania—more fruitful than the Shenandoah! Never touched by the plow!" He sold his land in the East, in Ohio, and in Tennessee. He sold to marginal farmers who'd burned up their land or simply had the misfortune to have had ancestors who had settled poor ground to start with. Nelsh sold his land in Scandinavia, and had great success there. Steamers leased by the Great Northern Land Company brought immigrants by the thousands, and no sooner had they landed in the New World than they were being whisked across it. When they reached the railhead, once again Jay Nelsh's agents were ready for them—ready to sell them plows, wagons, staple foodstuffs, sod cutters, grain drills, harnesses, even the horses they would need to turn the earth.

And once they were settled down on their little patch of earth, peering across the barren ground, five miles from the nearest neighbor and five thousand miles from their homeland, they became Jay Nelsh's constituency. Without the railroad bringing goods to the East, hauling their crops back to the population centers, these farmers could not survive. Without the hope of news from Europe, without the excitement of agricultural discoveries, they could not thrive. They needed the Great Northern, and they elected their first legislators with that purpose in mind.

But the plains had few legislators, and the Great Northern had powerful enemies, men who hoped to get more from the ruins of a railroad empire pulled down than from a link connecting civilized Minnesota with civilized Seattle.

There were fresh rumors of gold in Alaska, and, if the nation was on the brink of another important gold rush, the port city of Seattle would benefit. And any railroad terminating there would benefit too.

These were some of the considerations that moved Jay Nelsh between his work table and the few short hours he snatched on his office couch. He'd never said it aloud, but he had thought it: he would sell his soul to complete the railroad. He thought of little else.

When Senator Welfleet had asked for a tour, Nelsh had been delighted. The senator headed a cabal of men who planned to pick the Great Northern clean after it failed to meet its deadline this year and passed into the hands of the receivers. Nelsh took the visit as promising a change of heart. Perhaps the senator and his colleagues had decided to bet on the railroad rather than against it. Perhaps they'd found a way to make more from the railroad's success than from its failure. Nelsh certainly hoped so, and he wasn't above offering a few special concessions to the senator to steer him. Land? Special rates for his goods? Access to certain mineral properties the geologists had located in the Black Hills?

The world would be much improved, Jay Nelsh thought, once the tenuous link to the West Coast had been completed. He was a rich man, a man with millions, but he was indifferent to his wealth. He had pledged all his money to his dream.

Mile eight hundred thirty. Seventy-five miles of track on a gradual upgrade winding through the spires and pinnacles of the badlands. Jay Nelsh never once saw beauty in the bizarre rocks and spires of the badlands. They were merely obstacles to his railroad.

Nelsh bent to his drawings, seeking some way, some shortcut, some little innovation that could make it all happen faster. His engineers sighed and straightened. "Let's get some coffee in here if we're going to go over the long grade again."

In the quiet parlor car, Selkirk stretched and flexed

his long hands. "We'll be at the railhead long before dark," he said.

The whiskey decanter sat at Senator Welfleet's elbow, half its contents gone. "I suppose that's your idea of civilization," he sneered.

"It's all the civilization we have to offer, Senator," Selkirk said, calmly. "Fargo's got a good hotel, Drucker's, and it'll be a nice change to sleep in a bed that doesn't sway from side to side."

"What the hell did we ever want with this country anyway?" the senator snarled.

There was no answer to that one. There never is when a man's in his cups.

Count Deleis spoke very good English, accented crisply, more British sounding than Austrian. He had been educated, the count explained, in English schools.

Unlike Senator Welfleet, his patron, the count was quite sober, having nursed one lone bourbon through the long afternoon.

Jake was back in the kitchen where the servants gathered. He never was awfully comfortable around the gentry.

The captain read from the pages of *The Detective Gazette*, which chronicled the pursuit of the Hole in the Wall Gang by the Pinkertons. The Pinkerton captain was quoted as saying, "Cassidy and the Wild Bunch will be behind bars by the end of the year. We have them pinned like a rattlesnake pinned by a stick."

Captain Newell regretted that. This late in the game there weren't very many outlaws left to hunt and fewer ways of making a name. Jesse James was dead, the Youngers were in the hospital at Minnesota State Prison, Sam Bass was dead, Hardin dead,

Billy Bonney dead, Jack Slade dead. Hell, except
for the Hole in the Wall bunch, there wasn't much
for an aspiring peace officer to look forward to.
Once he and Lizzie Nelsh were married, he'd be
promoted to vice president of operations, but the
captain had always been a lawman and never wanted
to be anything else. With Lizzie's dowry he might
just light out for the Yukon and the gold rush. There
should be plenty of thorny characters north of the
Forty-fifth.

Where was Lizzie? She was rather unlike the
captain's usual choice in women, slighter than he
preferred and much less buxom. If the truth be told,
her inheritance attracted him more than her person.
She was no bigger around than a stick. The captain
expected nothing in bed. Lizzie Newell would be a
pure woman who'd dislike sex as much as common
trollops revelled in it. That was the captain's view
and his excuse for continuing to frequent those same
trollops whenever he could do so discreetly.

"Is Lizzie with her father?" he asked.

The senator smirked, wrapped his hand around his
glass, and took a tiny bird sip.

Selkirk looked away.

"Where's Slocum?" the captain demanded.

The senator's smirk grew. "I hope you can be
persuaded to join us in a friendly game once we
reach Fargo," he said. His smile was oily.

"Surely. Nothing I'd like better. Where is John
Slocum?"

The senator's pleasure at revealing Slocum's where-
abouts was ruined by Elizabeth Nelsh's reappearance
through the rear platform door. Captain Newell caught

just a glimpse of John Slocum leaning against the rear rail.

Elizabeth's normally pallid face was flushed and her hair was mussed. The captain jerked to his feet. "Lizzie," he called.

She ignored him, put her handkerchief to her lips, and hurried past the servants' quarters and the kitchen to the sanctuary of her bedroom.

The captain rushed after her. Though she'd closed the door, she hadn't locked it, and he came inside after the most perfunctory knock. "Lizzie? Are you unwell?"

The compartment was flooded with light. Light shone through the window and threw bright patterns on the far wall. All the bedclothes were on the floor in a heap, and the bed was covered only with white muslin sheets. "Lizzie, haven't the servants been in to make up your room?" he asked. He took her arm in his big hand.

"I did not want the servants," she said. "I wanted my curtains opened and the windows opened. I do not wish to be smothered in bedclothes."

She wouldn't look at him. He began gripping her arm a little harder than was strictly necessary. She pulled away from his grasp and made a face. "I do not recall giving you permission to maul me," she said. "Is this how I can expect you to behave after we are wed? Bursting into my room?"

Captain Newell's face was a study in confusion. "But . . . I thought . . ."

"You thought! You thought! Captain, I doubt you have ever had one thought in your entire life that wasn't quite conventional or given to you by someone else." She hadn't meant to go that far.

"You've been talking to that ruffian, Slocum."

She shook her head no, but it was a lie. Once again he took her arm. He squeezed, this time deliberately, because he wanted to hurt her, to teach her a lesson, to show her who was master. Her face went white with the pain but her voice was bell-clear. "Captain Newell," she said, each word as distinct as a death sentence, "if you do not release me and leave my bedroom, I shall cry out. I will tell my father you have molested me, and he will be glad to have you put off the train."

He let go, but his pride wouldn't let him give in altogether. "And who," he asked, "would he find to put me off the train?"

"I expect," she retorted, just as sweetly as could be, "someone could be found."

He stormed out of her compartment, mad as hell. The little train was just pulling into the Fargo yards, past the cranes and trackmen's coaches, past the flatcars loaded with rails and ties. Captain Newell went directly to his own compartment, much smaller than Elizabeth's, and checked the loads of the Smith & Wesson hammerless he always carried under his jacket. If John Slocum thought he could cuckold J. P. Newell, captain of railroad detectives, Slocum had another think coming.

The loads gleamed like shark snouts in his revolver. Angrily he grabbed for his riding quirt. He would lash John Slocum publicly, if he must; he was that angry.

But, alas, Slocum had left. Neither the senator nor Selkirk knew where the man had gone. The senator dared a laugh at the captain's furious face. "I expect you'll have plenty of time, Captain," he said. "Ain't you proud you have a rival?"

Later, very much later, Elizabeth Nelsh came out of her bedroom and marched directly to her father's office. She wore an emerald-green gown and her small collection of her late mother's jewels, and she carried a parasol in her right hand. She knocked briskly.

Jay Nelsh ran his hand through his hair and stared at the apparition that confronted him. "Lizzie?"

She smiled. "Elizabeth, if you please. After all, I am not a child."

"No. No, indeed, you're not."

"I believe we have an engagement for dinner."

"We have?"

"Yes, Father, we have. Dismiss your engineers—" with a smile to these worthies that quite took the sting out of her words—"and get dressed, and you may escort me to Drucker's dining room."

"Oh. I'll take you to dinner, surely. But I'll need time to finish here."

Her smile never wavered. "Very well, Father. I shall go by myself. If you do not wish to accompany me and protect me from whatever street ruffians might accost an unaccompanied lady, that's fine. Apparently you love your trains more than your own daughter."

The engineers coughed, adjusted their collars, and made themselves scarce. Nelsh sputtered but found himself rummaging through his trunks for something as dressy as his daughter's garb. Just minutes later he was escorting her to the handsome carriage that waited beside the car. Selkirk rode the box. Nelsh had a few letters to dictate. Perhaps Lizzie would be more comfortable if Nelsh were to ride beside his secretary, who could take some notes.

She gave that same assured, sweet smile. It never occurred to Nelsh to wonder where it had come from, but he was quite under its power. "My name is Elizabeth, Father. Elizabeth. Don't you find it a lovely name? If you ride with your secretary, I shall walk. I'm quite determined in the matter."

Nelsh sank back into his seat. His mind whirled, considering what he would do when he returned to work after this wretched dinner was over.

"Do you see that man, Father?" Elizabeth pointed at an odd-looking character. This particular character was a half-breed who worked various medicine shows as a fire eater and often lit a wand or two in the street in hopes of attracting some free drinks.

Nelsh didn't really see him. "Yes," he said, "of course."

Elizabeth pointed out some horses she fancied. Nelsh was losing his train of thought but he leaned forward to see and agreed that the animals were mighty handsome.

"And here we are at Drucker's." Elizabeth clapped her hands together. "Hasn't it been fun? Oh, Father, you don't know how I miss it when we don't get a chance to talk together."

"Yes, of course." Nelsh was out of the carriage and onto the boardwalk and Drucker's doorman had the wide oak door open for him before he realized Elizabeth hadn't accompanied him. He helped her out of the carriage and she was quite gracious. "Why, thank you, sir," she said exaggeratedly, in imitation of a Southern belle.

Drucker's was the best hotel and served the finest

food for five hundred miles around. It was crowded, but when the bell captain saw Nelsh he gave certain orders and the two sailed to a table which had been vacated and cleaned with astonishing rapidity.

Nelsh had seated himself before he noticed that she still stood. Blushing, he rose again to help her with her chair. He felt as though he didn't know his own daughter. As though he never had.

Though he rarely took spirits, Nelsh didn't object when his daughter ordered wine. And he laughed when, for a second, her new sophistication failed her as she tasted the red wine and made a face. "It's bitter," she said.

"Anything wrong, sir?"

"Oh, no, no. Just bring us a bottle of Monopole champagne. I hear bubbly is just the thing for fine ladies."

The waiter, who assumed Nelsh was with a young lady friend, winked and leered. Nelsh thought the whole evening was so funny that he didn't even object to the impertinence.

He saw his daughter in a new light. Perhaps she could be a help to him, instead of a burden to be pawned off on the first suitable husband. Jay Nelsh was not really capable of regret—his eyes were fixed too firmly on the future. But if he had been, he might have felt that regret now, for all the years when they could have been closer.

The dinner was elk steak, baked potatoes, and some late-season tomatoes. Generally he ate better in the privacy of his own car, but everything tasted fine to him tonight and he attributed that to Drucker's chef.

Replete, over coffee he turned his gaze to the

other diners, examining them, and thought—a rare thought for him—how interesting life was, how interesting were his fellow pilgrims.

The dining at Drucker's Hotel took place in one forty-foot room that doubled as the hotel's ballroom. The walls were white and the ceiling, of pressed tin squares, was also painted white. On three sides a balcony held overflow diners. John Slocum sat at one of the balcony tables, alone except for the Winchester laid across the nice linen tablecloth and a cup of coffee. His havana smoldered in the ashtray at his elbow. When Nelsh's eyes met his, Slocum allowed himself the slightest nod, so slight, indeed, that none of the other diners would have guessed at any connection between them.

Slocum rarely moved in his seat and never touched his coffee. He sat the way a red-tailed hawk sits on the branch of a big spruce tree, waiting for movement in the grass. His eyes searched every man who entered the dining room and the Winchester that lay under his hand had one up the spout.

One of the reasons he had hurried from the train was for a much-needed trip to the gunsmith. Slocum's long guns were still under arrest in Gull, along with his horse and his packhorse.

Nelsh felt a real wave of relief when he spotted the green-eyed man sitting so quietly above him. He'd been hearing the rumors of hired killers for six months now, but recently these rumors had become uncommonly persistent.

He ordered a cognac after dinner, which was not a usual habit. It would fuzz his mind slightly, he thought, and he wouldn't be able to continue working with his engineers. But this night, for once in his life, Jay Nelsh didn't give a damn.

Other diners were pressed by their waiters when they finished their meal. Other people were waiting to be served. But nobody pressed Jay Nelsh. Nelsh felt so good that he ventured a few weak jokes. He told the old one about the track foreman named Finnegan. "So," Jay Nelsh concluded, "he sent this telegram back to headquarters, 'Off again, On again, Gone again. Finnegan'."

Politely, his daughter smiled. She was feeling awfully good, as if she'd broken through some invisible but oppressive barrier.

Nelsh signaled the waiter when Senator Welfleet spotted them from the doorway and, without invitation, made his way over.

A chill went down Jay Nelsh's spine. He'd been having such a splendid time and Welfleet's arrival spelled the end of it. He could do business with men like Welfleet, but he would never be at ease in their company. Honestly, when he looked at it, he was more comfortable with men like Slocum.

"Hello, Jay. Enjoy your dinner? Lizzie."

Elizabeth let the informality whip right past her. She didn't care whether this gross hot-air balloon knew *anything* about her.

Without invitation, Senator Welfleet sat on a chair grunting. He snapped a lucifer, mouthed his cigar, bit off one end, and spat it onto the floor before firing it with the sulphur match. He puffed clouds of smoke. Elizabeth used her handkerchief to cut the fog.

"Jay, you mind if we talk a little business?" he asked.

He did, but he wouldn't say no. "Elizabeth, why don't you go on upstairs? Bring a drink to Mr. Slocum."

She resented the dismissal. Dismissals were for children, after all. But she did want to sit and talk some with Slocum. She wanted to show him her transformation.

When Jay Nelsh saw her safe upstairs, heading for Slocum's table, he asked mildly, "Business, Senator? Have you decided to accept some of my . . . concessions?"

"You know, Jay, I got to hand it to you," the senator said. "I would have bet a million dollars you wouldn't come close to mile eight-thirty before snowfall." He laughed ruefully. "In fact, I have bet several million on just that premise."

Jay Nelsh watched his opponent's face. Though the lips smiled and the cheeks were merry, Senator Welfleet had eyes with about as much kindness as broken glass, and they never blinked. "Perhaps," Nelsh suggested, "there's time to cancel your bets."

"Perhaps. Or perhaps I could persuade you to slow down a little, let the railroad miss its deadline. The Great Northern would go into receivership but what goes into receivership, Jay, also comes out, shorn of its debts and of the poor saps who've invested in it. The railroad would still be built—after a brief delay, of course, to satisfy propriety—and who better to build it than you?"

"I see. I had hoped . . ."

"I'd changed my mind? Jay, even if I could back down now, I have too many friends involved in this. I'm afraid that if the Great Northern doesn't fail, then I shall. Would a seat in the Congress interest you?

There are larger concerns than your railroad, you know."

"Yes," Nelsh said. "Perhaps you should return to those larger concerns quickly, lest they fall into disarray, lacking your firm guidance."

"Think about it, Jay. I'd hate to take a 'no' answer back to my consortium."

"I'm very much afraid that's the answer you will have to give them."

The sloppy smile got big enough to make a painless dentist glad. "Fine, then. We do not see eye to eye. Perhaps on some later issue we shall find ourselves aligned on the same side. No reason for us not to be friends."

Jay Nelsh could think of two or three perfectly good reasons, but he didn't want to antagonize the man any further. He put out his big hand. "Future friendship," he said.

"Yes." The senator's hand was as clammy and cold as his eyes, but he shook it vigorously enough.

For some reason his eyes strayed to the balcony, where he expected to see Elizabeth and John Slocum in earnest conversation, but their table was empty.

"I suppose you wouldn't mind a few hands of cards with me and Captain Newell," the senator suggested, "just to show there's no hard feelings."

"All right," Nelsh said. "But let's keep the stakes small. I'm not a rich man, you know."

The senator laughed and paid the waiter over Nelsh's objections. He steered Nelsh rather hurriedly out a side door of the dining room into a hall that was empty except for John Slocum standing in it.

And Elizabeth Nelsh who held a Winchester rifle across her body. Shocked, Nelsh hauled up, his jaw dropping. "If she's gonna be with us, she might as well be useful," Slocum explained quietly.

Fiercely, his daughter clutched the brand new '73. "I mean to help, Father," she said.

"Come along, sir," the senator urged. "They're waiting in the billiard room."

"Slocum?" Nelsh said.

John Slocum stepped into the dark, dim room first, ahead of the man he was meant to guard. Trailing the party, Elizabeth held the rifle with fierce determination and grimaced like a warrior.

They had rented the room for their private game. It was quiet inside the dark-paneled room with the big green tables. They played at a round table in the back. All the men played except John Slocum, who bent over the billiard table. The faint clicks of the ivory balls and the quiet voice of Elizabeth who leaned against the table to watch, were the only sounds from that part of the room.

Slocum locked the front door and admitted the waiter personally when anyone ordered a round of drinks. The senator ordered a great many rounds and Count Deleis ordered more than his share. Jay Nelsh wasn't drinking, nor was the count. Selkirk took one modest glass of spirits and seemed intent on having it outlive him. The captain drank pretty heavily.

The stakes weren't anything much—table stakes; bet and raise limit of ten dollars. The stakes weren't much to Jay or the senator. In the first half hour the captain was through his ready money and had borrowed two hundred dollars' worth of chips from the senator.

"Slocum, have a drink," the senator suggested.

"Naw. I gave it up," Slocum replied without rising from his shot.

"Oh, nonsense. This cognac is really superb."

"You drink it, then."

The senator returned to his game, shuffled carefully, and dealt one down, one up for five stud. Without checking his hole card, he bet five dollars. Captain Newell, slack-jawed, peered at his low pair and met the bet. "That's what I like about poker," the senator beamed. "It tests your wits."

When the count handled the cards, everybody knew the pasteboards had fallen under the spell of a master. His hands blurred, shuffling, reshuffling, flicking the cards to the players.

Jay Nelsh wasn't much of a poker player, but the stakes were low enough that he really didn't care. He made his reasonable bets, called when he thought the count or the senator didn't have it, and generally lost. He was here for politeness' sake. If it hadn't been for the count and the possibility of attracting some European capital he would have left after an hour.

As the count dealt, John Slocum came over, chalking his cue. The deck riffled and jumped. The cards flicked out to lie precisely in front of every player. Slocum groaned. "Ah," he said, "surely you're not gonna do that!"

The count picked up his cards and examined them before lifting his eyes to Slocum's. The count's eyes were bland, dark, unexpressive.

"Sir?" he asked.

"I said you ain't gonna do that." Their eyes locked for a moment until the count dropped his discards and announced that the dealer would take two.

Captain Newell was in over his head, and his head wasn't very high up. When he lifted his glass to his lips he almost missed it, and his tongue came out to lick some moisture off his chin. He was betting erratically. Sometimes, with a sly look, he'd bet high in the opening stages of a hand before anyone had their cards, only to fold when he saw his last one. Sometimes he underbet what looked to be, and was, a surefire winner. He gave IOU's to the senator, who said, "Any time, Captain. Any amount."

At first the captain was a jolly drunk, betrayed as intoxicated only by the sly meanness of his bets. As he continued to lose, he began to get rough. He'd throw down his bad cards so some of them fell to the floor. He cursed his own hands—"Damn, what can a man do with a pair of eights?"—letting anyone else who held such a pair know that he had no chance to improve.

"For God's sake, man," Nelsh cautioned him.

"For God's sake, man," the captain sneered back at his boss.

The count said, "Play cards."

Selkirk took a look at his hand and upped the bet by ten dollars.

The cards simply fell out of Captain Newell's hands and he stared at the way they lay, some face down, some face up on the table.

"You out?"

Slocum came up behind the big captain, caught him under the armpits, and dragged him to an over-stuffed armchair. "I think we could say he's sitting this one out,'' Slocum remarked. The captain sat, eyes wide open, rigid as a corpse.

Selkirk was winning about as much as he was losing. Nelsh was up. The senator was down. When the waiter tapped on the door again, Slocum gave him orders for another bottle of cognac and a big pot of coffee.

There was something quite hypnotic in the game, as though greater things were being decided than the modest wagers. Nelsh felt as if his eyes were stuck open. His daughter had appropriated another over-stuffed chair and was curled up in it, leaning the rifle against the arm. When she was asleep, Slocum tip-toed over and moved the rifle so she couldn't knock it over in her sleep.

Slocum returned to his solitary billiard game and the bets, calls, and raises were punctuated again by the click of the billiard balls.

Nelsh's watch said three A.M. He stifled a yawn. ''Gents, it's awful damn late,'' he said.

''Oh, you can't call it quits now, Jay. You've got too much of my money.'' The senator checked his own watch. ''Let's give it another hour, then we settle.''

The count's hands froze on the cards. His hands were white, the color of lard, and practically hairless.

''And let's play some real poker for a change. Say a hundred-dollar bet or raise. Will that suit you?''

Nelsh expected Selkirk to demur but the secretary had a couple hundred dollars in winnings and maybe he figured to be lucky.

Five stud. Nelsh had a king showing and another in the hole. He bet the limit and picked up another king before the dealing was done. With just four playing, three kings was an awfully nice five-stud hand, and it would probably win. But someone beat them with three aces. The count scooped up the pot. "Much obliged!" He laughed.

And as the cards rolled out, Nelsh began to feel sure the count was cheating, dealing himself hands that were too good to be true. Maybe he even had a few up his sleeve. He won almost every pot and he did win every big one.

Nelsh didn't stop to wonder why this clumsy cheater had lived so long. He was genuinely puzzled by the man's actions and, in a rather scientific mood, wanted nothing more than to catch him at it.

The count was dealing. Nelsh saw him, plain as anything. He grabbed the count's hand. "Those cards are coming off the bottom," he announced.

No more click of billiard balls.

"Release my hand, sir," the count said icily.

"But you were dealing your cards right off the bottom of the deck. Everybody else's are coming off the top and all yours off the bottom. I saw you. I'll bet a hundred dollars the last two or three cards on the bottom here are mighty special."

Nelsh was sprawled halfway across the table. Oddly, the count wasn't watching. He was looking over Nelsh's shoulder to where John Slocum stood. He released the cards. Then, quite deliberately, he slapped Nelsh across the face. "Sir," he said, "I will wipe this slur off my name with your blood."

"Not right now, you won't," John Slocum drawled. And Nelsh didn't need to look to know that Slocum's hand was on his pistol butt.

The cards scattered everywhere. The count scooped his winnings into his hat. "Shall we say eight A.M.

with pistols? You will give me a chance for my satisfaction?''

Nelsh was slightly dazed. "Oh, hell," he said. "Oh, hell. What's all the commotion about?"

The senator reminded him, rather gently, that most men don't care to be called card cheats.

"Oh, hell. Oh, Christ."

The count stormed out of the room and, after a moment, the senator followed him. John Slocum racked his billiard cue. Nelsh rubbed his face. "What in God's name can I do?" he asked.

"If I were you, sir," Selkirk suggested, "I would avoid this duel. If I were you, I'd get on the car and return to Minneapolis."

"I have a railroad to build!" He turned to the quiet man behind him. "Tell me, John, what would you do?"

Slocum shrugged. "Ain't much of a hand at giving advice," he said.

"I'm asking you."

"Where I come from," he said, "man'll kill his own snakes."

"I see." Nelsh heaved himself to his feet. "I'm no great shakes with a pistol, and I'll need all my steadiness. Selkirk, will you be my second?"

"Yes, sir."

Strangely, Nelsh did sleep for a couple of hours. He sank like a stone as soon as his head hit the pillow, and the servants had to shake him awake at dawn.

His eyes roamed around the familiar contours of his combined office and bedroom. It all seemed strange to him, fragile, impermanent.

The knock came before he was completely dressed.

His daughter was in the doorway. "Oh, Father."
She'd been asleep when she was carried to the coach
the night before. "Selkirk told me. Must you do this
terrible thing?" she asked.

"I fear I must."

"Oh, Father . . ." She rushed into his arms and
hugged him so hard he could feel all her strength.

"Don't worry, honey. I didn't wait all these years
to get to know you just to have it last only one day.
I'm too practical for that."

She tried on a brave smile, but she couldn't hide
her tears.

Nelsh called Selkirk into his office, where he
spent most of an hour hammering out instructions.
He was just putting the finishing touches on his will
when a servant announced Senator Welfleet.

Welfleet was quite cheerful. "Ready, Nelsh?" he
asked.

"So you mean to go through with this thing."

"It's regrettable. If we called it off either the
count would be a cheat or you would be a coward."
He didn't make it sound particularly regrettable. He
was hot for the showdown. "We'll drive out past the
old steamboat landings. It'll be quiet enough there,
and private."

Nelsh's party elected to follow in their own carriage.
Slocum rode up on top with the driver. A pale
Selkirk rode inside with his boss and offered optimis-
tic counsel. "Surely it'll be called off. Surely it
will."

It was an awfully pretty morning with just a touch
of fall in the air. Clouds were high above them and
the pale sun scarcely warmed the earth. In another
two or three days the ground would show frost. Jay

Nelsh was jolted by the realization that he, precious and unique Jay Nelsh, might not be here in a couple of days to see that first frost.

Eyes grainy from too little sleep, he shuddered to think that, with a lifetime of work still before him, he could soon be dead. It was unthinkable.

They passed the rotting wharves that had once served a flourishing river traffic. The railroads had put the riverboats out of business. And the rivermen's skills, the intimate knowledge of bars and currents, snags and flats, where were they now? At one time they must have seemed important knowledge. Beyond the last wharf he could see the single derelict funnel of a small steamboat that had mouldered right at its moorings. He looked away because the sight made him sad. He created a mental picture of his two bright sets of rails turned red with rust and overgrown. It couldn't happen. The United States would always need its railroads.

The dueling field was an ordinary piece of bottom-land, banked from the river's irrational surges. It was a ten-acre pit, lower than the river and lower than the slope that rose out of the bottom. Some farmer had made hay on this field not so very long ago and the grass was no more than three inches high. It glistened with dew and morning spiderwebs.

How intricate life is and how beautiful, Nelsh thought.

The senator's coach waited at the far end of the field. A stranger climbed out of the coach with the senator and the count. He carried a little black doctor's bag and had a severely disapproving look on his face.

The two parties walked toward each other. The

principals stopped some distance from each other and the senator shook hands with Selkirk. Loudly, the senator asked, "Are they quite irreconcilable, then?"

Nelsh wanted to shout that he didn't care. He didn't give a damn if the Count Deleis was a cheat or not. But his mouth was too dry to utter the words that might save him.

"The count offers you his personal dueling pistols. Etiquette demands that you pick a pistol and deliver it to your principal."

Selkirk pulled a dueling pistol from the long plush-lined box. The senator took the other one to Count Deleis.

"The principals will begin back to back, take twenty steps, turn, and fire. Are there any questions?"

"Yeah." It was John Slocum speaking. He had his arms crossed and one of his legs cocked and generally could not have appeared more relaxed. "Count? Are you gonna go through with this? Is it really what you want?"

The count glared at him. The senator lifted one eyebrow. "If there are no further questions, we can settle this matter on the field of honor."

As they came together, Jay Nelsh studied the count's face, but he saw nothing there except the man's determination. The count wouldn't meet his eyes. They lined up back to back. Through his coat, Nelsh could feel the other man's warmth. A meadow-lark set up its trill upslope somewhere. Oh, to be that bird, free to go, free to fly!

"Are you ready, gentlemen?"

Jay Nelsh couldn't have felt less ready. He'd rarely handled a pistol, never a European dueling pistol.

The bird's-foot grip felt awkward in his hand. He supposed it would feel more nearly right when he had it leveled.

"Step off, then. One, two, three, four, five . . ."

Nelsh's back went suddenly cold, and he felt awfully exposed. He'd stop at twenty, turn, raise the pistol, and point it at the count. He'd fire. That was all there was to it.

"Seventeen, eighteen, nineteen, twenty."

He turned then, quite smoothly, and the gun lifted to the end of his arm, and the mote that was Count Deleis danced on his sight. Perhaps he'd have the first shot; the count was waiting.

The mote in his front sight disappeared, fell out of view. The shot echoed up and down the river, scaring a couple of wood ducks into the air, and their honking echoed the report. Confused, Jay Nelsh lowered his dueling pistol. He released the hammer he'd cocked just a moment ago. The count was sitting on the grass, pistol at his feet, clutching his midsection.

Jay Nelsh hadn't fired. He came closer reluctantly. His pistol hung from his long right arm like a brick.

A trickle of smoke lifted from the muzzle of John Slocum's Colt.

Jay Nelsh was, quite literally, speechless. Slocum had cut down the count without so much as a warning. He had drawn and fired, as though murder was the most natural thing in the world.

The count toppled over onto his side, the blood welling helplessly through his fingers. He made an awful sound, something between a belch and a cry, and his legs jerked out straight and trembled.

John Slocum said, "Curly Bill, I told you not to do it."

"Who?" Nelsh was stupefied with confusion. He didn't understand anything.

"Count Deleis is a two-bit tinhorn name of Curly Bill. I played cards with him a couple times in Tombstone. He was one of the best mechanics. Second card, bottom card, false cuts, recuts—you name it and Curly Bill was your man. He never did have too much objection to back-shooting, either."

"You murdered Count Deleis," the senator said to Slocum. "I'll see you hang for this."

"Wonder why so many men want me hanged? Men hardly get one look at me before they start saying my neck's too short."

Nelsh said, "It was a fight between him and me. You shot him down without mercy."

"No more mercy than he showed you. He was about to murder you."

"But . . ."

"He let you catch him cheating. If he hadn't wanted to be caught, you never would have spotted him. Give me that pistol."

Jay Nelsh handed it over.

"You'll hang," the senator huffed furiously.

John Slocum said, "So they trapped you into this duel and then they meant to cut you down. I warned Curly Bill. I warned him."

"It's murder."

John Slocum lifted Nelsh's dueling pistol and aimed it right at the senator's chest and pulled the trigger. The report was quite loud and the senator's face was astounded.

"Like I said, they were gonna murder you. They didn't bother to load one of the pistols with a bullet, just powder and cap. Then they made sure you got the pistol with no bullet in it.''

Nobody would have believed him, but there was the incontrovertible evidence of Senator Welfleet who, shot point-blank, was quite intact, though extremely uncomfortable.

Nelsh couldn't help grinning at his old antagonist as the man shucked his clothes, cursing a blue streak. Slocum's unbulleted black-powder pistol hadn't wounded him, but it had set his shirtfront on fire.

5

"Oh, that senator thought he was a dead man! The look on his face when Slocum pressed the muzzle to his breast and touched it off!"

Old Jake was positively dancing with glee and the grins on the black servants' faces were wide and white.

"Oh, he was mad. The pistol was plumb full of black powder and a wad. It didn't have no bullet, don't you see? But that wadding was burning and when it touched the senator's nice ruffled shirtfront—oh, my!"

"And Miss Elizabeth? How did she take it?"

"Well, she was afraid for her father, of course. When Slocum cut down that rapscallion would-be count, Miss Elizabeth didn't bat an eye. Anything, just so her daddy was safe."

At this, the three black heads nodded agreement. One servant stuck his head out of the kitchen and reported, "Mr. Nelsh and his engineers are hard at it. Mr. Slocum and Miss Elizabeth, they just talking."

"Get out there and ask them if they want anything," the head steward ordered. "And what happened then, Mr. Jake?"

Jake settled back against the serving counter. He took another sip of his whiskey-laced coffee. He was a happy man. "Well, once the senator got the flames beat out of him, he pulled his shirt right off. Oh, he swore he'd take revenge. He said he'd do plenty bad things to Mr. Nelsh and promised worse for John Slocum. He said he knew a bad man, a man who ate the likes of John Slocum for breakfast. He said he'd set that man after Slocum, sure. The doctor, he was working on that fake count, but there wasn't much for him to do beyond putting the pennies on his eyes. He was dead through and through. The senator tugged the doctor away, saying he wanted something for himself, and I was glad to see the last of them. They never bothered with the count. Once he was dead he was no further use to them, so Mr. Nelsh hauled him into Fargo and John Slocum paid for the man's box himself."

The servant returned. "Mr. Slocum say he don't lack for nothin'. Miss Elizabeth wants the iced tea with a sprig of spearmint in it."

Nelsh's car carried its own ice, which it replenished at each provisioning stop. Nobody used it in drinks except for iced tea, a relatively recent fad in Chicago, though its critics asserted that the practice of dropping ice cubes in drinks was barbaric.

Jake drank more spiked coffee and continued his story. "Mr. Nelsh, he was pretty grateful, and he said Slocum could have most anything he wanted for savin' his life."

Jake was a good storyteller. He knew enough to pause while everybody conjured up the rich presents and favors a man like Nelsh could deliver.

"John Slocum just kind of grinned at him. You know that grin of his. He said he'd been thinking about going south. 'Runnin' before the bad weather,' that's how he put it. But now he was thinkin' of stayin' for a while. I think he's beginnin' to get interested in Miss Elizabeth." Jake nodded sagely, agreeing with his own wisdom. "Though I don't know whether she'll have him or not, Captain Newell and her bein' engaged and all."

"The captain's with Mr. Nelsh now," one of the servants noted.

"Well, if he had the sense of a half-wit, he'd be sittin' back here with his girl," Jake observed. "Otherwise he's gonna lose her."

Jake was half right. Elizabeth had lost much of her feeling for Captain Newell. He'd been a fool the night before, manipulated and tricked. This morning he'd been lost to drunken sleep. And he owed so much money to the senator that his loyalties were compromised—and this, finally, was the unforgivable offense. Captain Newell was not completely bound to her father's interests, and Elizabeth Nelsh could not forget that.

John Slocum fired a cigar. His Colt lay disassembled on a piece of chamois cloth. He'd cleaned the gun very carefully and charged the empty chamber. Two rifles, a Winchester 44-40 and a .50 Sharps, lay beside the Colt. Though he had covered the table with newspaper, the two rifles looked incongruous in the room.

The guns were new and stiff and covered with petroleum jelly, the most viscous product of the new wells in Oil City, Pennsylvania. The stuff smelled awful and it wasn't as slick as sperm oil, but it would keep a weapon from rusting. Laboriously, Slocum cleaned both rifles, inspecting each tiny spring, pawl, and cam for manufacturing flaws, insuring against bad luck.

Elizabeth broke the silence. "What will we find at the end of track?"

John Slocum turned the Winchester hammer piece in his hand. He tested the sear with his thumb. Slick enough. "Hard to say," he replied.

"I fear trouble. Several years ago the train was attacked. I kept my blinds drawn so I wouldn't be too upset, but I was upset just the same."

"Uh-huh." Deftly he reinserted the hammer. He wiped the self-tapping screws with a piece of linen cloth. His cigar smouldered in the crystal ashtray beside him. He tightened the screws and tested the lever and hammer action. The rifle had a longer barrel than the carbine and was quite a bit more accurate. It wasn't so handy on horseback or in brush, but he figured to be doing his business from the train. The rifle snugged right into his shoulder. Not too bad a fit. If he had time, he'd slip a shim between the stock and the steel butt plate. His arms were longer than most and the gun was a short fit.

He held the rifle up to the girl. She warded it off with upraised palms.

"Learn how to use this," he said, "and you can keep your blinds up all the time. A woman with a rifle or pistol is just as strong as a man with a rifle or pistol."

"They are extremely . . . unladylike."

He allowed himself a quick smile. "Yes, Elizabeth, they are. It's more ladylike to shriek and faint or contract the vapors when danger threatens. But then the danger comes on and does what it means to and there isn't anything you've done to stop it except to say please don't. It's just like any other job. Once you set your mind to it, you'll do a better job of protecting yourself than anybody else will."

She shuddered and looked away. "I hate guns," she stated.

"Uh-huh." Slocum started work on the Sharps. Miss Elizabeth returned her iced tea to the kitchen twice. Once it was too sweet and then it was too strong. She watched Slocum's hands. They were big hands, with calluses on both thumbs, and small cuts and scars on the knuckles. The fourth finger of his left hand jutted out, as if it had been broken and badly set. The hands were sure, very sure, and Elizabeth found herself wondering how it would feel to be touched by those hands. She put down her third glass of iced tea with a thump. She hadn't really wanted it anyway. "You Southerners have a reputation for gallantry toward women," she said to Slocum.

"I heard that myself." He repeated the same moves with the Sharps, throwing it to his shoulder, taking a slow, swinging bead as if a bird were flying across the rear of the car. He shook his head. "Sharps never was much use unless you had a tripod," he said. "Awkwardest gun ever invented. But it'll drive nails for you." He put both rifles down on the carpet and pulled out the ammunition. He pouched the Sharps ammunition and punched a full dozen brass cartridges into his ammunition belt.

"Wouldn't a gallant man protect a lady?"

He ignored her. It was a question boredom had fashioned. "You want to come with me?"

She gave him a quizzical look.

"Change into rough clothes and we'll go up to the locomotive," he said.

It was a surprising request but, in all the times she'd ridden the car, she'd never gone up to visit the engine that pulled it. The novel suggestion intrigued her. "Wait a minute." She hurried to her room. She had an old riding outfit somewhere.

Jay Nelsh saw the excitement in his daughter's face when they passed through his office. "You be careful. Watch your feet," he told her.

Nelsh was a railroad man, first and last. If his daughter wanted to crawl around a train moving at sixty miles an hour, he didn't see anything particularly unnatural in it.

Slocum climbed the swaying ladder up the tender, slinging the rifle carelessly from his hand. Elizabeth counted the rungs above her—eight—and saw the world blurring past at the edge of her vision and beneath her feet. Her heart picked up tempo to accommodate her fear.

The tender loomed above her like some overhanging cliff, some black metallic thing. "If you're afraid, go back inside." Slocum was gone again.

Clumsily, Elizabeth Nelsh clambered up and, using the cleats lined up for that purpose, she edged across the tender, focusing very very intently on the next step, her next hold, and the position of her body. The locomotive was really pouring it on. A steady stream of cinders and soot landed in her hair, stung her face, and tickled her nostrils.

The engineer and fireman were so baffled by her arrival that they couldn't do anything but stare out the windows of the rushing locomotive, quite ignoring the girl who'd just climbed out of their coal bin, looking as filthy as any ragamuffin.

Slocum leaned his rifle in the corner just beside the big brass pressure gauge. He stuck out his hand. "Name's Slocum. John Slocum."

The engineer was called Murphy. The fireman, who mumbled his name, was either Gleason or Keenan—something like that. Both men wore the high-peaked railroader's cap and owned genuine Illinois timepieces, accurate to a minute a month.

The cinders passed overhead, the wheels drummed, and the firebox glowed like the guts of hell when the fireman loaded through the little door. The wind blew Elizabeth's hair. Slocum insisted on introducing her to the trainmen. Both of them removed their hats and scuffed their feet. They'd seen the boss's daughter a thousand times, but she'd never seen them once.

There were trees in the creek bottom, cottonwoods mostly, and a few quaking aspens. The creeks were all dry and would stay dry until early spring snowmelt. Jay Nelsh's railroad shot across the barren ground like a sword, infinitely long, infinitely flat, dwindling to a point on the horizon.

The trainmen didn't talk much among themselves. When they had unexpected company, they became mute. The fireman stoked his fire. The engineer made a dozen minute, unnecessary adjustments. He pulled the steam cord because he hoped Miss Elizabeth would like it.

She thought it was too noisy, awfully shrill, and the cloud of steam vapor wasn't awfully pleasant either. She laughed anyway and clapped her hands, just like the child the engineer expected her to be. John Slocum gave her a disgusted look.

The engineer spoke to Slocum and Slocum alone. "You expect we'll run into trouble at the end of track?"

"Dunno."

"You're Mr. Nelsh's bodyguard."

"Yep."

"Job pay good?" While the engineer talked he made adjustments, proving how terribly important he was to the operation of the train.

"Fair."

"I got a brother. He's in the Chicago police. He . . ."

"Tell him don't bother. Tell him it's safer in Chicago. Of course, there's all the free travel."

"Ha, ha," the engineer said.

Elizabeth Nelsh looked at the countryside and tried to think how it would look when the farmers came and transformed the earth. A herd of pronghorns jumped up, racing for the middle distance. She dreamed of cities rising on the plain. She was very much like her father. The other glistening track looked like a steel ribbon beside them.

"You got any weapons up here?" Slocum asked.

The engineer had a Smith & Wesson Bulldog in his lunch pail. The fireman had nothing.

"If anything breaks," Slocum said, "I want you to back this train out of it. No questions. First bullet and we make dust. If there's trouble out here, it'll be planned."

The engineer didn't say anything.

Elizabeth clambered back onto the tender. Her feet dangled onto the coal pile. She was higher than the locomotive's roofline underneath the smoke. John Slocum joined her and caught his rifle between his knees.

"Isn't it glorious?" she said, meaning the speed, the wind, the power of the locomotive, the wind in her face.

Slocum checked his watch. "Yeah," he said. "We

should reach end of track in half an hour. If you want to be ready to help, I'll show you how to work the Sharps."

She tried on a smile but it didn't fit. She looked away. In a very small voice she said, "I'll just retire to my room."

"Suit yourself, Lizzie."

Her head snapped around as if it was on a swivel. She glared. Stiffly, she clambered back on top of the tender and made her careful way back to the private car. It was much easier this time.

Five minutes out, Slocum returned to the locomotive cab. The cab was lined with sheet iron, and there are worse armors.

The engineer was the hooting news of their arrival, his head stuck out the side window. They passed the first of the tents and rough shacks that made up end of track, that constantly shifting reference point of the railroad. He put a round into the Winchester's chamber and the fireman sighed. The engineer eased the throttle back a stop, then another.

No sign of trouble. The men came out of their tents and scratched their bellies or shaded their eyes, but nobody raised a hand against the hurrying locomotive. One or two men, off-duty foremen, waved in the friendliest manner.

The engineer backed the throttle and kept his eye on the pressure gauge.

The sun-faded tents at end of track were military tents. They'd been tattered, patched, and tattered again. The last item in the budget of the financially strapped railroad was housing. The men had thrown together temporary shacks, just walls with a canvas roof draped over a ridgepole. End of track moved west every week or so, and everything in the camp was portable.

The point of the Great Northern Railroad accommodated several thousand workers, surveyors, engineers, and supervisors and met their needs. There were sutlers' stores where the men could buy everything from heavy canvas pants to suspender buttons to trade whiskey so poor they dared not sell it to the Indians. One of the sutlers provided an awning, and a row of barrels to sit on, a plank bar, and even a rudimentary free lunch: sliced and dried buffalo hump, and venison jerky.

Big new tents right beside the right-of-way stored railroad provisions. Everything valuable enough to tempt a thief was inside these long warehouse tents, guarded by two of Captain Newell's men who were armed to the teeth.

The blasting powder was stored in a dugout on the far side of the tracks. Some Swedish fellow, Nobel, had invented a new explosive substance called dynamite. Dynamite, pound for pound, had ten times the power of blasting powder, but it was delicate stuff. The chemicals leaked and solidified if it stood in one place too long, and it was the job of a couple of men who were longer on courage than on sense to turn every stick once a week.

Slocum moved from one side of the cab to the other, cat-nervous, trying to spot enemies before they moved. Nothing. Nothing. Nothing. John Slocum raised his hand and returned a wave or two.

The engineer looked at him triumphantly, as though John Slocum had imagined the danger.

They stopped beside the work trains: three locomotives, flatcars, coaches, a caboose.

Men called questions to the engineer: Did they haul track, ties, repair parts, spikes? He answered no to all of them.

When they learned Jay Nelsh was the train's sole cargo, they went back to their own pursuits, quite unimpressed. Slocum slung himself down.

He saw Elizabeth Nelsh come out, but he didn't go near her.

Elizabeth was arguing with Jake. "No," she said. "I don't need you following me about. If I want to leave the car, I shall do so, and neither you nor Captain Newell can prevent me."

"Your daddy ain't gonna like it," Jake said stubbornly.

"My daddy . . . my daddy has enough on his mind. He shouldn't be worrying about me. I am armed now and I can take care of myself."

Propelled purely by principal, Elizabeth Nelsh stepped onto the main street of end of track. In her purse she carried a revolver. She had simply demanded that Captain Newell provide her immediately with a suitable weapon.

When he demurred, claiming it was his job to protect her, she said, "Be that as it may, Captain. If you protect me as ably as you have protected my father, I cannot hope for a long or happy life. I'd as soon be protected by John Slocum."

He offered her his spare hideout pistol, the little Smith & Wesson gamblers and tinhorns and prostitutes were beginning to call the Lady Smith. It was light but well made and easily fit a whore's muffler—or Elizabeth Nelsh's purse. She spun the cylinder, inspecting the rounds in a professional manner.

"Where'd you learn to do that?" Newell demanded.

"Know the workman by his tools," she replied sweetly.

The weight of the pistol was a comfort to her. The camp was full of workmen. Half the shift was off duty. Plenty of tanned and work-hardened males showed the kind of terrible curiosity that can quite fluster a good woman. She walked proud, her head high. Because she needed to invent a reason for her walk, she became a tourist, studying the details of the camp smithy as though she'd never seen a black-smith before.

"My," she said, "that anvil must be awfully heavy."

The smith set down his hoof rasp, stepped to his anvil, and lifted it chest high and over his head, grinning like a bear at the beautiful young woman.

He smelled like a bear too. Elizabeth backed away. "My," she said. "My goodness."

The men outside the sutler's stared at her. They thought she was a new whore. Why else would a woman be at end of track? But something in her manner restrained their coarse suggestions.

The goods wagons crashed along in the greatest hurry, as though armies pursued them. The men eyed her, stopping work, conversation, and drinking, to examine this apparition. Elizabeth reflected that independence was as much a curse as a blessing. There were some things a woman shouldn't have to endure.

The camp follower's accommodations more or less reflected their prices. Some of these women slept in open-ended barrels no better than doghouses and rolled in the dust with any man who had two bits. The fancier girls had small tents of their own.

John Slocum stood outside one of these tents and, if he hadn't had a girl on his arm, Elizabeth would have joined him. She'd had quite enough of independence.

Elizabeth didn't know the girl, but she had no doubt what she was. She lowered her eyes and didn't utter a word and backed away, hoping mightily she hadn't been seen.

In a moment she was out of sight of John Slocum and that . . . that—that— As many men stared at her on the way back. She didn't notice a thing.

"Hello, Lena," Slocum said.

Lena's jaw dropped. She gaped. Her head whirled around dangerously. Here was the man who had given her both fleeting fame and, later, shame when he fled his hanging. The madam had been angry with Lena, cut her price, and forced the worst of the customers on the poor girl. Lena took the first train to end of track, where she hoped to do better as an independent.

"You!" she gasped.

"What's the matter, Lena? Not glad to see me?"

She took a quick swing at him right then, and if he hadn't caught her hand she would have done some damage to his eyes. "You bastard!" she hissed. "You murdering bastard!"

"Take it easy, girl. Take it easy." Wrestling with her, he contrived to push her back through the flap of her tent. It might have been rape. It looked like rape, but none of the onlookers on the street were of a mood to interfere. When a woman made her living on her back, she lost the usual chivalrous protections.

The tent wasn't bad. Before she left the Abilene

House, Lena had taken time to loot a few purses, and gold dollars went pretty far out here. She had a great steamer trunk at her bedside. In another trunk, upended in the corner, her dresses hung. Lena had attached a small mirror to this wardrobe trunk and had even found a few late-blooming prairie flowers for the milk-jug vase beside her bed. Two camp chairs faced each other beside the trunk, with a bottle of whiskey and two glasses between them. Lena had set up a class operation. She was prettier than most of the camp whores, and she meant to be the richest.

"Damn, Lena, I thought you'd be glad to see me." Slocum wore a farmboy's grin and had his hat in his hands. Rather coldly, she opened her blouse. Her breasts were pink, with her long nipples pointing slightly outwards. She held her breasts like offerings, but her face was full of contempt.

Slocum sat down, poured himself a straight whiskey, sipped, and coughed. "Christ, woman," he sputtered, "can't you do better'n this? I'll tell you what. I can get a couple cases of good whiskey off Nelsh's private car. I'll do that." He nodded at his own proposal.

Angrily, she covered herself. "I don't need your whiskey," she sputtered.

"You like blind men for customers?"

"What do you want with me?" Lena wasn't a very good woman, but she wasn't stupid, and she didn't think John Slocum was here to enjoy the pleasures he'd sampled before. She plopped herself down in the other camp chair. "Do not lie to me," she said.

Slocum sipped again at the whiskey and again

made a pained face. "You heard anything about men wanting to kill Jay Nelsh?" he asked.

He was sprawled so easily, so comfortably in her own tent. *Her* tent, with its whiskey and flowers, was her own—something more than just a whore's crib. "Why would I tell you?" she asked.

He stood up then, and he wasn't smiling at all. "What's your price?"

"Five dollars. Gold."

The gold coin flashed as it spun through the air, and landed, dead quiet, on the counterpane.

She opened her dress, head to toe. He never looked at her body. He laid his curious green eyes on hers and the hair on her arms stood up. She rubbed her arms to warm them. He dropped his shirt behind him, tossed his heavy gunbelt on her steamer trunk, and nearly toppled her bottle of whiskey. He didn't care where it fell. His eyes never left hers.

He took her cold arms in his hands and pressed them, and her arms warmed, but she felt a little faint.

He was a customer, nothing more. Five dollars gold—nothing more.

He dipped his head to hers and his face looked cruel and distant but there was nothing distant about his breath when he breathed into her mouth and his chest hairs scratched her nipples.

"Take off your pants," she said. "Cold." Meaning his belt buckle against her bare belly.

She let the gown fall off her shoulders and it fell somewhere. When he pressed against her he was hard, and she reached down and took his cylinder in her hands, remembering it like an old and intimate friend.

His hands were in her hair, going through her fine-spun hair, and she was slipping down, sliding helplessly down to his belly, and then she was on her knees. She took him in her mouth because she wanted him, because she cherished him. His hands were in her hair, caressing the very top of her head, where she had no nerves at all, but she felt it. Her breasts flattened against his legs and her head nursed on him and she was vaguely shocked when he pulled out of her mouth. Her spittle glistened on the head of his cock and she looked up, so far up, and though she didn't say it, she meant, "Why?"

He lifted her gently and she kissed him then, her eyes full of tears. She was trembling, too, her thin shoulders shaking in his hands. He lifted her then, held her out, and slid her onto him as if she were a scabbard. She clung to his neck and he lifted her, his hands under her buttocks, lifted her and lowered her. That was his only motion. His cock was guided only by that motion.

"Oh," she said as he rocked her. "Oh, God!"

It started in her chest, just beneath her aching breasts, and flowed down. She let down her love as he ground upward into her, making the deep connection.

Her belly rippled against his, her hips twisting and drawing his seed, until he flooded her rain with his rain. It was a shock when the two rains met and mingled and washed, and she clenched her muscles to hold them in.

Directly he set her down as gently as he had picked her up. She looked into his eyes and saw that he liked her, that he would not forget. Maybe it was the whore's cynicism that expects the man's eyes to hold nothing but contempt, but her heart yearned, wanting to be a gift, and only her old hard brain, older than her years, held it back.

"So," she said. "We didn't even rumple the bed." She picked up her robe and draped it around her shoulders. She felt exposed.

He sat down again and took another bit of whiskey. "I guess it just plain can't be improved," he noted.

She wrapped her garment around her waist and tied it tight. She felt sticky between her legs and her breasts were cold. She almost wished they had used the bed. She almost wished they could have lain together, warm under the blanket. It was going to be a long cold winter. It wouldn't be so cold with a man to share it with. She'd do her work and he could have some of the profits. She'd never had a man of her own before. Perhaps this man would be her first. But she didn't know how to ask him. "Why don't you put your clothes on?" she said.

"Surely." He dressed, and set the angle of his pistol just so. "You interested in that whiskey?"

She wasn't, really. She was interested in him. But she said, "Yeah, I'll help you find out what you want to know." She was thinking about the cold weather and the snow outside the tent, and one rough bastard after another, with none she could love.

The early dusk was falling across the prairie when the two emerged from the tent. Lena disappointed a couple of admirers who'd been waiting patiently outside.

Shifts had changed thirty minutes ago and the men were lined up before the water barrels, collecting water for their evening meals or just sluicing down, swapping jokes and lies. A haze from the cook fires hung over the camp and lanterns hanging in the tents winked their yellow welcome.

With John Slocum at her side, Lena made her way through the camp. She'd made a few friends in Gull. She spoke quietly, promising favors for information. Slocum stayed out of it.

Finally she stopped at the sutler's, perched on a barrel, and ordered a bottle of rye whiskey, the special stuff.

It wasn't that special, but it was better than what she had in her own tent. John Slocum sat beside her and they put their heads together.

"There's fifty men here in this camp who don't work for the railroad," she said. "They ain't tinhorns or sutlers or camp cooks, and they sure as hell ain't in my line of work. There's a few people wondering what they're doing here."

"Uh-huh."

"And your friend, the senator, is in camp. Nobody knows what he's doing."

"He meetin' with anybody?"

"I don't know."

"Where can we find him?"

She shrugged. As the dusk deepened and the evening star sailed across the pale blue of the sky, they strolled the streets at end of track. Lena wore Slocum's jacket and tucked her hair up under her hat so she wouldn't have to refuse anybody. Tomorrow night she'd want customers again.

The early-to-bed crowd went to bed. The early-to-risers followed shortly. That left the ones with the strength left to raise hell, and the camp got rowdy. The workers were common laborers, uneducated and strong. They set up dice games in the dirt outside their tents and card games within. They lined up in whore alley and quite a few were disappointed that Miss Lena wasn't receiving tonight.

Lena asked her questions, and the answers were short.

"There's an Indian in that big white Baker tent over there. Indian's been there two days and hasn't come out except to take a piss. The senator's due any minute."

"All right, Lena. Thanks. You go on back. I'll be by later." John Slocum bought a laborer's jacket right off the man's back and a soft woolen cap from another. He let his pant legs down over his boots and in a few moments he looked like a gandy dancer, though maybe a little taller than most.

He crouched outside the rear of the Baker tent and pulled his soft cap over his forehead.

They didn't try to disguise their arrival. They were that arrogant. All the Indian's caution was nullified when the senator and his men rode through end of track, big men on big horses.

They tied up their horses and went right in. John Slocum was ready to rise from the shadows when he saw another shadow slipping toward the tent. He froze. The man paused at the entrance and looked around carefully. His eyes moved on past Slocum, swept by again, and he vanished inside, scarcely ruffling the canvas flap.

In a second John Slocum was pressed against the canvas, flat on the ground, one ear engaged.

"Chief." That was the senator's deep voice. "Are you ready to fight?"

The Indian's voice sounded odd, very slightly

different, like he was moving around. "And if we do not fight?"

"Oh, our deal's still good. You and your people can return to your home." There was something Slocum didn't like in the senator's voice. Something alarming.

"Senator?"

Now where had Slocum heard that voice before? He knew it from somewhere. . . . But now he was rolling away from the edge of the tent as quietly as he could, seeking shadows where he could rise to his hands and knees, because such alarm had overwhelmed him that he had been propelled backward.

A shadow appeared on the canvas of the Baker tent, a blot of the clear silhouettes in the lantern light.

More softly now, the Indian said, "What is your plan, Senator?"

In the next instant a knife ripped through the canvas and buried itself in the dirt beside the tent. Blindly the Indian had thrust through the canvas wall and buried his knife in the exact spot Slocum had occupied moments before.

The Indian's face appeared in the triangular tear his knife had made, his eyes blinded by lantern light seeking an enemy in the dark.

Slocum had never seen a face quite so fierce, unless it was the face of a wolverine he'd killed in northern Montana. Pure ferocity, pure rage. The Indian's eyes were light-blinded. Slocum had to keep reminding himself of that as he backed into the darkness, careful not to make a single sound. The Indian had heard him or sensed him when he hadn't made a sound, and now he had his ears cocked to catch Slocum's noiseless retreat.

Still in the shadows, Slocum moved back into the street, back to whore's row, like any other gandy dancer intent on the same errand.

He recognized the other voice he'd heard, the furtive man who'd slipped in last and spoken just the single word "Senator." Selkirk, Nelsh's secretary. The accent was unmistakable.

He hurried back to the private car. There was plenty of work to do before morning.

6

Captain Newell hurried through the poorly lit streets, sober, well dressed, and glad. He wore his best dark suit buttoned tight over a vest that encased his chest and belly like horsegut cases a sausage. His bowler was set far forward on his head, tipped that way in jaunty indifference. God, it was good to be alive. Alive and in love.

He dipped his head through the tent flap and poked through. Rough-looking men were playing stud poker by lamplight.

"Cap'n Newell."

"Evening, sir."

His own men, toughs hand-picked to provide security for Jay Nelsh's enterprises. He had thirty good men and true, out here at end of track. Once he had Elizabeth Nelsh as his lawfully wedded wife, he'd expand their numbers. "We've got work," he announced.

The man shuffling the cards ceased his riffle. Another one folded his hand and tossed it in the middle of the table. Every eye was on the big captain of detectives.

"We'll want every man jack armed with pistol and rifle. Those who prefer goose guns, bring them too, but everybody will be expected to turn out with a rifle."

The dealer rubbed his eyes. He sneezed. "What's the trouble, Cap'n? Labor organizers again?"

"No." Newell backed out of the tent. "Jackson, I'll want you to alert the men in the other tent. Send a crew to the sutlers' and bring the boys back sober enough to be of use."

Once more he strode down the makeshift street, his bulk and presence clearing the way for him. Track layers and gandy dancers stood aside, parting before this proud, important man who forged through like an arrogant gunboat.

Supplies. The railroad stores were guarded by his men. He found it satisfying that the stores should be guarded by his men. The world had revolved like a roulette wheel and the ball had fallen into his slot.

This morning— Oh, this morning didn't do to think about except, he thought sternly, to remind himself how far a good man could fall. He awoke, lying where he'd passed out, in a chair in the billiard room. He woke with a stiff neck and a bad stomach and a head that felt as big as a ripe watermelon. He remembered enough of the poker game to know he owed Senator Welfleet the better part of next year's salary. That hadn't made him feel very much better.

When he got some water splashed on his face and rolled out to the front porch, the carriages were just returning from the duel. The sun hurt his eyes. Everybody ignored the captain of security. Only old Jake would even tell him what had happened.

Caught up in the rush to get back on the train and out to end of track, nothing more was asked of him than getting his own sick self aboard the train. He supposed the senator wouldn't be traveling with them again. Hours later, he decided he didn't owe the senator a red cent because Count Deleis had been cheating and, according to those sober enough to notice, the cheating had been at the senator's direction.

But this morning had been a long time ago. He shouted into the recesses of the big railroad tent: "Charlie—Joe! Captain Newell here. Get your lazy butts out here."

He took a few minutes to dress them down, snarling like an angry dog. He concluded, "If you useless pieces of duffel don't snap to, you'll be looking for honest work before morning. Charlie, you get over to the explosives and bring back a case of dynamite and some caps. Be careful. Joe, see to the foodstuffs. There'll be thirty men on that train, and some of them will be hungry. Bring the spirits chest. I'll keep the key. I'll want plenty of linen bandages and some carbolic for wound disinfectant. I'll want five hundred rounds each of .44-40, .45-70, .30-30, .25-20, .35-45, and a case of those paper cartridges for the Sharps. Lanterns and a couple gallons of kerosene. A bottle of laudanum. Let's get ready for a fight!"

"Who we fighting?"

Captain Newell allowed himself a little smile. "Whoever comes at us," he said. "Hop to it."

The whole camp knew something was up. Men roamed the streets of the tent town.

Captain Newell enjoyed their curiosity. He enjoyed not telling them a damn thing. He enjoyed his victory.

The men sent to guard the trains missed one of the work trains which chugged on down the eastbound track and paid no attention at all to the shouts and waving lanterns of Newell's men. A brown hand clenched a slat in the train's only car. The great headlight of the work train dwindled in the distance, grew tiny, and finally disappeared.

When John Slocum fired his quirly, the light threw the harsh planes of his face into sharp focus.

Captain Newell strutted over, reluctant and proud. "We'll be ready," he announced, man to man.

Slocum nodded at the eastbound track. "Did you see who took that goods train?" he asked.

"No. It was pulling out before my guards reached it."

"That's too bad." Slocum picked a fleck of tobacco off his lower lip. "It'll mean trouble down the line."

"That's what we're preparing for," Newell said, rather more stuffily than he'd intended. Now that his services were important again, Newell was more friendly. He didn't hate John Slocum. Hell, when this was all over and Elizabeth and he were safely wedded, there'd be a place on his staff for a man as quick thinking as Slocum.

Elizabeth surely was a changeable woman. All morning while the train rattled toward this place, coming west from Fargo, she had ignored him. Old Jake would talk to the captain, but nobody else paid him much mind. Elizabeth looked right through him. All right, he'd made a mistake, got drunk when he shouldn't have, and had failed to protect her father. Every man was entitled to one mistake, wasn't he? But she had eyes for nobody but this Slocum. It didn't make the captain feel any better. He figured old man Nelsh would fire him as soon as he gave it any thought, and now his fiancée was treating him like a piece of furniture. It was a low point, all right.

But later, when darkness fell, everything changed.

Elizabeth followed John Slocum into the tent city, and whatever she saw there did not sit all that well. On her return, her eyes cast around the private car until they met Newell's and she came right over, filled with life. She said she was sorry she'd treated him so roughly. She knew he had a heart of gold and would never look at another woman. Bewitched by the return of all the opportunities he'd thought were snatched forever beyond his reach, he agreed. As a reward, she gave him one of her decorous little kisses, which wasn't all that great in itself, but served notice to everybody in the private car what the real state of affairs was and would continue to be.

Later on, John Slocum completed the captain's triumph by asking for his help. "I can't organize our forces without you, Captain. I don't know when we'll be hit, but a real wolf pack of the senator's thugs are gonna attempt to take Mr. Nelsh's life. And I surely intend to give them pause."

Perfect. His fiancée and he reunited and his value to the railroad reestablished. It made a man feel forgiving. "John," he said, "I think we're pretty well prepared."

"I wish I knew how many men were on that goods train."

Newell shrugged. "What difference does it make? With our forces we should be able to take care of any attempt on Mr. Nelsh's life. We'll be able to put thirty men on the train, armed fighters all."

Slocum looked at him for a very long time before he shook his head. He ground his quirly out under his boot heel.

The cars clanged together as they coupled onto the

new train they were making up in the makeshift
yards. First the big Pacific locomotive and tender,
then a flatcar loaded with railroad ties. Slocum figured those ties would stop a .30-30 dead in its tracks
and discourage a Sharps. Then came a boxcar, and
finally the private car.

Men loaded provisions and the ammunition into the
private car. The lanterns cast funny yellow shadows across the hard-packed roadbed. Men spoke
quietly, hustling the goods aboard. Other men stood
apart from the loading crew. These men carried
rifles, hip high or across their shoulders, loaded and
ready. In the front of the car a light glowed behind
the drawn blinds where Jay Nelsh and his engineers
did their work. The engineers thought the preparations were ominous but Nelsh ignored them, driving
them for more plans, more details, faster work.

Neither Slocum nor Newell recognized the man
heading toward them. The stranger walked like another railroad stiff. He didn't have the look of a
gunman at all.

"Either of you gents named Slocum?"

"Who's lookin' for him?"

The stranger said, "I'm supposed to give him a
message from a girl down in the whore row. Lena,
her name is. Pale-haired gal. She says some gents
are hangin' around and she said you should come."
He scratched his hat. "That's all she said. She said
it'd be worth four bits for me to bring the message."

Slocum tossed him half a dollar and the man
scuttled off.

"He'd already been paid," Newell said to Slocum's
back. Slocum had already started. His thumb was
unfastening his hammer thong. Newell hurried after

him. Breathlessly, he said, "He was one of the senator's men."

"Likely he was."

"Why'd you pay him?"

Slocum had very little patience for talking that made nothing happen. He shrugged.

"It may be a trap," Newell suggested. Slocum's legs were longer than his, and the captain had to take a step and a half for every step the taller man took.

"Likely is." Slocum left the main street and passed between a couple of tents. "We'll come at 'em from the side. It ain't much edge, but it'll have to do."

Captain Newell had more than his share of human faults, but cowardice was not among them. He drew his Colt and kept it at his side. He was sweating. When Slocum drew up, Newell nearly stepped on his heels. Slocum put a hand up for silence.

He couldn't tell if anyone was inside the tent or not. A couple of late lovers stumbled down the dirt street, arms around each other, giggling. Lena, was not one of them.

Slocum whispered, "You go on in ahead. Walk right into the Baker tent over there. If Lena's in there—she's a blondie, a little shorter than Elizabeth Nelsh—bring her on out here. Maybe we can take her without any gunplay."

Not many people were still awake. Most of the whore's tents were dark. Most of the activity was over by the yards, where the men still worked to get Nelsh's train made up.

"Newell," Slocum advised, "when you go into the tent, wait a while before you come out. Give it ten, fifteen minutes. If there is anybody interested in Lena, it'll give me a chance to spot them."

Captain Newell jabbed Slocum with his elbow. He was being sly. "How can I be with a woman for just fifteen minutes, John? It'll damage my reputation." Chuckling over his own witticism, Newell crossed the dirt street, avoiding the ruts, looking very much like a late lover. In the darkness, his Colt was invisible against his pant leg.

Lena lay fully clothed on her camp bed, hands behind her head, staring at the canvas ceiling. She looked at Captain Newell with some distaste. "I'm closed, mister," she said. "I'm too damn sore to take on another stud right now."

It wasn't the time or the place but, rather unexpectedly, Captain Newell found himself wanting her. Her indifference to him made her all the more attractive. Give him half a chance and he'd teach her a thing or two. Quite forgetting Elizabeth, quite forgetting his promises, he grinned at the girl. Maybe later. "John Slocum sent me," he said.

Well, she sat right up then, and her eyes lost their indifference. "John? Where is he? Is he all right?"

"Maybe yes, maybe no." Even with the little time available to them, Captain Newell wanted to bring the girl a little lower. It was natural with him, almost an instinct.

"Please," she implored, "tell me."

Loftily, he pulled back from her then, prissy as an offended virgin. "Oh, Slocum's alive. At least for the moment."

"What do you mean?"

"He's out there in the shadows waiting for your enemies to show themselves."

"What enemies?"

Newell knew perfectly well that the message they'd

received was a fake, but it was nice to have that fact confirmed. "They used you as bait to bring us under their guns," he said.

"John?" She started toward the tent flap, and only Newell's tight grasp on her arm held her.

"We wait for the enemy to show his face."

When she jerked her arm out of his grasp, he added, "That's how Slocum wants it." He checked his watch. "Ten minutes," he announced.

She was pretty agitated, and her small breasts were in motion under her loose gown.

"Ten minutes," Newell repeated. Then he made an indecent suggestion.

"I'd just as soon screw a donkey," she said.

"I would have thought one man's money was as good as another's."

She wasn't paying full attention to Captain Newell; she didn't give a damn about him. If only she knew! If only he could tell her! He felt the slight deeply. She didn't care at all about his bright prospects, his ambitions, or his bravery in the face of danger. After all, hadn't he come to rescue her? Slocum wasn't alone. But he said nothing. He just sneered at her for ten minutes, checking his watch, watching the hands make their laborious circle. Though his ears were cocked, he heard nothing—not a sound.

"Since we may have to make a run for it," he said at last, "I'd suggest you put on some sturdier shoes."

She looked at her feet, at the little slippers she wore. "I'm a cheap slut, mister," she said. "I ain't got no sturdy shoes." She stood up then, opened her trunk, and found a dress, simpler and less provocative than her occupation demanded. She turned her back. Captain Newell glimpsed her long back, her small buttocks, her long legs. His cock jumped against his pants and he hated the idea that any other man had ever taken her, been with her. He hated her for all the men who'd slept with her. Most of all, he hated her indifference to him. She got into the gingham dress and wrapped a shawl around her shoulders. She kicked her slippers aside. If she had to run, she'd run barefoot.

Outside, in the shadows, Slocum had spotted six of the senator's men, and he had no doubt there were more within gunshot. He had a good patch of shadows. The moon was half full, more nuisance than light, the shadows were like ink pools. Down the road another weary whore doused her lantern while her last customer went home humming to himself, cheerful and loose.

He walked past Slocum in the shadows. Slocum could hear the captain and Lena talking but he couldn't make out what they were saying.

It was tricky slipping around the tents. A man could trip over a tent or a guy rope, and the commotion would bring the guns down on him, sure as death.

Two men stood to the left of Lena's tent, quite still, barely visible in the dim glow of the light inside. Another man was on the right, a big bastard. It looked like he had a long gun in his hands, a shotgun or a rifle. Him first.

Slocum could hear the sounds of men breathing inside the near tent, the sounds of someone snoring. Somewhere down the line, a sleeper called out. Slocum hunkered down on his heels, quite comfortable, his ready Colt across his body.

Once, in the Wind River Range, John Slocum had waited, wounded and half frozen, behind the bole of a downed Douglas fir for eight still hours for the Crow buck who'd ambushed him to show himself. When that brave came to claim the scalp that was rightfully his after seeing no motion, not even chest motion, for the eight hours, John Slocum had killed him fast.

Waiting fifteen minutes was nothing. He noted a couple of shadows on his side of the street.

Because she didn't want to sleep with him, Captain Newell pushed Lena out ahead of him. She stumbled and fell and he was a dandy target. One pistol flashed, then another, down the street. Newell dropped to one knee and returned the fire.

John Slocum let loose at the big figure with the long gun. That worthy hollered and dropped.

Rapid as a racer snake, Lena crawled across the street. Slocum risked a call and she tracked him on her hands and knees. The firing was heavy but inaccurate. The senator's men put bullets into the road beside Lena and into the tents across the street, where they killed one sleeping man and badly wounded two others. Slocum killed another man and sidestepped his own muzzle flash. He grabbed Lena. "Down, stay flat," he breathed.

They had hit Captain Newell. Even from here Slocum could see the darkness spreading on the captain's leg. Slocum fired twice, then shifted quickly to the left. His bullet brought a yell but he was half blinded by gun flashes and couldn't tell how much damage he'd done.

"Newell! Make for the train!"

Newell raised one hand in agreement and, limping, started down the street.

Men were pouring into the street now, armed railroad workers, mad as hell.

Slocum holstered his empty pistol and hurried Lena deeper into the shadows. They were soon invisible and the shots that sought them made cracking sounds when they passed.

Slocum and Lena reached the safety of the train, but Captain Newell wasn't so lucky. His almost perfect day ended abruptly when a bullet found his heart and he toppled into the dirty street, dreaming no more.

The death was reported to John Slocum, just as if Slocum had inherited the captain's mantle.

"All right. Get back to work. I want that flatcar stacked tight with ties."

Lena had lost her shawl escaping from the tent, and now her arms were crossed to keep her from shivering.

The sky became the dull gray of false dawn. The gray spread across the sky, dismal as rain clouds, but Slocum could see a little better. The vent for the car's kitchen discharged fine odors. Slocum reloaded the Navy, all six cylinders this time. If he didn't miss his guess, that pistol would be worked hard today. "You been a whore a long time?" he asked the girl.

Lena shrugged. "Am I gonna get killed here at end of track?"

"I doubt it. I figure they were just using you to get at me. If you're worried, you can come with us to Fargo. We'll get shot up some. If we get through, Nelsh means to return to Chicago. He'll be safe back in Chicago."

"And you?"

"I never gave the matter much thought. I been thinking of going south. Texas, maybe. Always did like that brush country down by the Rio Grande."

"Maybe I'll go south."

It was his turn to shrug. "Pretty soon it'll be light enough to roll. I didn't want to move until we could see them coming at us."

One of the servants stuck his head around the door to announce breakfast.

Slocum rubbed his stomach. "I ain't real hungry, but I suppose I better eat. You?"

Lena marveled at the lush furnishings. She gaped at the paintings and said, of the picture over the mantle, "Why, that looks like the real horse is here in this car!"

Elizabeth was at the table with Selkirk. The table was set for four with fresh flowers and crisp linen. "Why don't you introduce me to your . . . friend," Elizabeth said coolly.

For someone who'd just had her fiancé killed, Elizabeth's manner was very cold.

"Lena . . . Elizabeth."

Lena tried a little, awkward curtsey. "Pleased to meet you," she said.

"Yes, I'm sure. She was as cold as sterling silver.

"It's a beautiful place you have."

The contrast of the two women was ridiculous. Elizabeth wore a gown worth three men's wages, and Lena's dress was clean but hard-worn. Elizabeth wore two jade pendant earrings with half-carat diamonds and had a hint of perfume behind her ears. Lena was barefoot and wore so much smeared makeup that she looked like a clown.

"We like it," Elizabeth replied to the girl's awkward compliment.

Slocum interposed, "Her life's in danger, Elizabeth. She'll travel with us as far as Fargo."

"In danger? How odd!" Elizabeth's arched eyebrows could have held up a railroad bridge.

"Yes. They were shooting at us."

Lena wasn't witless. She wanted to be polite to this awesomely rich young woman, but her patience wasn't endless.

"They shot Captain Newell, you know."

"I met Captain Newell." Lena would have lied, invented some kind words for the captain she didn't lament, but she thought better of it.

"I was the captain's intended," Elizabeth said with great dignity.

Lena's smile was quite involuntary. In another fashion, she'd been the captain's intended, too, but it was nothing she'd care to brag about.

Having disposed of the little tramp John Slocum preferred for some unaccountable reason, Elizabeth turned to the man himself. "I believe you wish to leave immediately. I've discussed the matter with Mr. Selkirk and my father. He can do his work much better here than back in Fargo. We admire your preparations, Mr. Slocum, but we do not feel they are justified."

John Slocum pulled back a chair and called to one of the servants. "Bring me and Lena some grub," he said. "I don't care what, just good portions." He moved his water glass and leaned across the table to repositon Elizabeth's glass. "I don't know what put the burr under your saddle," he said, "but I'll explain a few things about our circumstances. We're here at end of track. As far as your father's concerned it's the end of the world." He pointed at her glass. "That's Fargo. Senator Welfleet can hire any number of killers in Fargo and send them after us one at a time or in whole companies. Sooner or later one of them is bound to slip by me, and then your father's dead." He stabbed his fork at Selkirk. "And you don't want to be listening too much to Selkirk, because he's working for Welfleet, same as Count Deleis was before I planted him."

The servant set down a platter. Lena wanted to start to eat but she waited.

Selkirk got to his feet. "Sir!"

Slocum laid his pistol beside his plate. He stabbed at an egg. The tines ran yellow. "Yeah, that's right. Last night he was with Welfleet and the worst-damn-lookin' Indian I ever saw in my life."

Selkirk bristled. "I'll ask you to retract that, sir!"

"Uh-huh. You'll ask me for a .36 caliber slug. I ain't in the mood to be humorous. I probably should cut you down right now but I'm hungry and gun play will spoil my breakfast. I believe you had better make tracks, Selkirk. Tell Senator Welfleet we'll meet again sometime, some place."

"I will not. This outrage . . ."

John Slocum cocked his Colt. "There aren't too many things I'll do for a perfect breakfast," he said. The pistol wandered very slightly. One moment its muzzle seemed to threaten Selkirk's right eye; the next moment it threatened the left.

He collapsed, like a suddenly deflated balloon. "My bags. I have clothing, personal papers . . ."

"I'd hate for my eggs to get cold," Slocum said. "Git."

So Selkirk made his unseeing way from the private car, past the world he'd known and subverted for so long, away from a world where he was every man's friend. He moved to a world where he was nobody's friend and had no man's trust or faith. Though it wasn't really cold, he shivered slightly. He would ask Senator Welfleet for the loan of a jacket.

The guards on the rear platform looked strangely at him, but they didn't know he'd been a spy. "Good morning," he said.

They returned his greeting. There were two guards on the rear platform, twenty-five men in the special flatcar. The senator would like to know that.

His life was changed forever.

Elizabeth Nelsh had been angry before, and the unmasking of Selkirk didn't appease her. Quite the contrary. John Slocum had been infuriatingly right about a man she'd trusted. Now he sat at her table, his grubby Colt smudging the tablecloth, placidly eating eggs and sausage. She hated his breakfast, hated the fact he could eat it. She hated the little tramp, too. The only thing she liked was the other girl's awkwardness, her inability to handle the table service. Elizabeth smiled at the girl the way a crocodile smiles.

The girl had seen that kind of smile before, and felt under no obligation to return it.

The first edge of the red sun crept above the horizon and the colors inside the car grew more alive as the light touched the crystal vase and the bright silverware. It softened the lines of Lena's too-thick paint and made John Slocum's face look weary and old.

The engineer blew an inquiring whistle. Slocum turned to the rear of the car. "We ready?"

"Yes, sir. Last of the men came aboard ten minutes ago."

"Horses?"

"Just like you wanted. Horses are in the boxcar."

"All the servants off?"

"Yes, sir."

Slocum dabbed his mouth with his napkin. He wasn't hungry; he was impatient. "Give him the high sign."

The brakeman's lantern swung side to side once, twice, three times, and the engineer hooted back. With luck, the train would be in Fargo by night.

With luck.

Slocum went forward to check his troops and their dispositions. Elizabeth found herself alone with the woman she hated most in the world. "We will take you only so far as Fargo," she told Lena. "If you have any idea of traveling farther with us, make new plans. Besides," she added, "there are already plenty of your sort in Chicago. You might say the market suffers from a glut." She made the word sound like the word it rhymed.

Lena gave up using her fork and took a sausage delicately between her fingers before nibbling the end. She wiped her greasy fingertips on the tablecloth. Again, dainty nip, dainty wipe. "Fargo's all right with me," she said. "Never should have left Fargo in the first place. Gull was bad. End of track is ten times worse. Men are animals, you know that?" She put her eyes everywhere but on Elizabeth."

Elizabeth found herself agreeing. "Yes," she said.

Now Lena did raise her eyes. "You're better off without him," she said.

Elizabeth's expression was puzzled.

"That captain. The bullet that took him in the heart was the best bullet ever made. He wasn't worth my little finger." Lena held up her little finger to illustrate. It was about the same size as the small sausages she'd been nibbling.

The train groaned and clanged and the mighty locomotive worked and started rolling. Outside the windows the khaki shades of the tent city slid past.

"Captain Newell was a man of honor, and he died trying to save you," Elizabeth replied acidly.

"Wasn't for John, he would have left me to rot. He wanted to have me, though. Oh, indeed he did."

Elizabeth hurled down her napkin. "Crude!" she snapped. "Crude, awful lies!" She stormed out of the car into her private compartment.

Lena shrugged and went back to the sausages. End of track vanished in a few moments, even before the train really got up speed. Lena was glad to see the last of it.

Idly she looked out the window and sucked the grease off her fingertips.

A rider flashed past her window, going much faster than the train. Some sort of Indian rider, a slight figure on a big horse, riding hell for leather, he was overtaking the train before it got up speed.

Lena had seen Indians in her life but they were mostly derelicts, drunken relics who hung around the trading posts and sutlers' bars. This was different. This man was as wiry as the strong horse he rode. Excited, Lena jammed her face against the window, trying to see the man better. He carried a parcel of some sort in his right hand. With a whoop, he hurled the parcel into the locomotive tender and ducked down beside his horse as it veered away. The Indian was plenty close but nobody fired on him. Nobody had really expected this kind of sendoff.

The parcel landed smack on top of the heap of coal and rolled onto the locomotive floor, where it was blocked by the fireman's boot. The wrappings were bloody and so was the thing inside. The fireman leaned outside the locomotive and lost his breakfast.

"Slocum!"

The lean, green-eyed man hurried forward in answer to the fireman's shrill cry for help. He climbed over the horse boxcar and the flatcar, manned with good men and true.

"What've you got here?" he asked.

The pale fireman indicated the thing with his foot.

"Oh, hell," Slocum said. He knelt beside the head of Captain Newell. The skull had been scalped and the cheeks flayed so his white teeth glistened front and sides. Slocum whistled. He turned the head once to get a better look at it. Then he rewrapped it and kicked the fire box door open. Before the engineer could interfere, he tossed the grisly bundle inside and shut the door.

Both fireman and engineer gaped with horror.

Reasonably, John Slocum said, "I could have buried it in the coal heap. Would you have liked that better? Get rifles up here, both of you. Next time you see some damn redskin riding alongside the train, drill him. You hear?"

The two men nodded.

"No need to tell anyone about this," he continued.

"Everybody knows Newell's dead. Nobody has to know what else happened to him."

The plan to shake Nelsh's men failed. Failed because John Slocum saw it for what it was: Indian magic, an Indian curse, an Apache trick. It was an Apache's work, cutting the cheeks away so the skull looked particularly horrible. And that face Slocum had seen last night had to be Apache.

John Slocum had spent time in Arizona Territory and had even scouted for Crook once or twice. But that had been against Comanches. He'd never fought the Apache. He knew them for savage, never-say-die fighters—perhaps the craziest and cruelist of the plains Indians. But what in god's name were they doing in Dakota, a thousand miles north of their usual country?

Selkirk, Senator Welfleet, and Apaches. It made a peace-loving man wary. Slocum sat on the back of the tender and cupped his hands around his quirly. Thoughtfully, he watched the smoke whip away from him.

As per instructions, the train moved at a steady forty miles an hour. Slow enough to stop if Welfleet's men had removed a rail or blown a trestle.

John Slocum felt the wind ruffling his hair, pressing the shirt against his back. If he was a smarter man, he'd probably drop off the train and start walking south. He shuddered, That damn head had upset him more than he thought. They called it the Indian sign for a good reason.

Behind them, Welfleet's men got the pursuit train ready for business. Unceremoniously, they stripped the gear, the equipment, and the seats out of two old coaches that had served as temporary shops.

The track gangs objected, of course, but Welfleet's fifty ruffians had them buffaloed. Selkirk said the instructions came directly from old man Nelsh himself. The track foreman complained and muttered but finally let Nesh's private secretary have his way.

The pursuit train was powered by two locomotives, front and rear. Last night the trackmen had had three locomotives and tenders. Once the pursuit train set off, they would have none. The men would have to push the rails to end of track on horse-drawn cars. Nelsh's foremen were as conscious of time passing as their boss was, and nobody wanted to see delays.

At Senator Welfleet's request, they skidded a heavy sheet of boiler plate onto the caboose. The plate, intended for a stationary steam engine, was a semicircular affair about six feet long and three feet high. It would provide quite a bit of protection for men lying down behind it.

Selkirk would ride with Welfleet, acting once more as a private secretary. It never struck him as strange that he should be doing the same job for Jay Nelsh's greatest enemy as he'd done for Nelsh, because Selkirk didn't really think of Nelsh, Welfleet, Slocum, or Captain Newell as real. He thought their fights were foolish and their enmities trivial. Selkirk's own ambitions and struggles were quite real enough. But other men had a certain insubstantiality as though they were part men, part wraiths, never quite so important as the stuff of his own dreams.

Selkirk had modest ambitions which he promoted ferociously. He meant to have a ranch, a herd of cows, a home, a wife, and children. He knew the spread already, a section in the Wolf Creek Canyon. It had been surveyed by the Great Northern survey-

ors and Selkirk, through an agent, already owned
options on the land he wanted. His childhood sweet-
heart still lived in Scotland, but they corresponded
regularly, and she was going to immigrate once the
railroad reached the land he'd described so lovingly
in his letters. That the railroad might fail, due in part
to his own efforts, and thus never reach the land he
wished to own had occurred to him as a possibility
and nothing more. As much as he was capable of
irony, he thought that was ironic, but Welfleet paid
him very well, three hundred a month.

Though the senator hadn't remarked on it, Selkirk
feared his pay would be reduced now he was out of
Nelsh's entourage. Selkirk hoped the senator would
forget to do this, in the heat of the pursuit.

Rough men were boarding the passenger cars.
Most carried long guns in each hand and wore a
brace of pistols. Some of them carried another pistol
or two, in shoulder holsters. They outnumbered
Slocum's crew by two to one. In the end, it would
be firepower that mattered.

The engineer whistled and the brakeman waved
his signal flag. The dapper secretary mounted the
steps of the caboose.

A couple of the senator's Indian allies shared the
caboose with them. The painted buck savages had
greasy hair, breechclouts stiff with filth, and crazy
black eyes. They understood the senator's orders but
they never spoke English in return.

It had been the senator's idea to scalp and flay the
captain of security. The Indians did the job with no
particular relish, but rapidly. One of them offered
the senator Newell's bloody scalp. The senator re-

coiled in horror. "Christ," he said, "what kind of savage do you take me for?"

The Indian shrugged and sheathed his knife. The scalp vanished into his possibles bag. A scalp was a scalp, after all.

The two Apaches rode upstairs in the little turret, jabbering and chattering in their heathen tongue. Selkirk was relieved to have them out of the way.

Selkirk took his place on the hard bench with his mahogany traveling desk. The box held paper, pens, extra nibs, and two bottles of india ink. The top, when folded back, made a fine writing surface.

"Will you have any correspondence this morning, sir?" he asked.

Senator Welfleet looked at Selkirk with distaste. A tool is one thing, a broken or useless tool another. "No," he said shortly. "No letters this morning." Unnecessarily, he added, "I generally don't find it difficult to write my own letters."

"Yes, sir." Selkirk wiped his pen nib and stored it back in the desk. "But surely a man of your stature requires competent help with his affairs?"

Welfleet lowered his brows. "Man I buy, anybody can buy," he said shortly.

Selkirk flushed to the roots of his pale hair. "As you wish, sir." He closed the lid of his desk and folded his hands.

Senator Welfleet prowled the narrow aisle of the caboose. He saw the legs of his allies propped against the turret ladder. He saw the hurt, sullen face of his former spy. Somebody would have to do for Selkirk once they ruined Nelsh. The train rattled and shook. They were traveling full tilt.

Somewhere ahead was Geronimo's train. Twelve

full-blood Apaches, engineer, and fireman were in the train he'd sent out last night before Slocum could prevent it. If the pursuit train failed to finish off Mr. Nelsh and his associates, the Apaches could do the job.

For just a moment, Senator Welfleet felt pity for the men he hunted down. He promised himself that he would take care of Jay Nelsh's daughter himself— just shoot her dead. He'd never let her fall into Geronimo's hands.

Selkirk broke into his thoughts. "What will you do with the Indians once they've done their work?"

Senator Welfleet smiled. "It'll be a tragic story. The railroad builder and financier, Jay Nelsh, dies at the hands of hostile Indians in Dakota Territory. A relief train manned by Senator Welfleet arrives too late to save Nelsh but not too late to punish the redskins."

"You'll kill them?"

Welfleet smiled. "Justice," he said. "True justice."

Selkirk tried an answering smile, but it started to slip off his face. What use would the senator have for him when the fight was over? he wondered.

Selkirk rubbed his chin thoughtfully. If that little ranch in Wolf Creek Canyon was ever to be claimed, he'd have to keep a close eye on whoever stood at his back.

He slid out from the cramped booth and said he was going up front to check on the men.

"Yes. Make sure they're alert."

The two gutted passenger coaches were lined with men peering out the windows, drinking, and making their boasts. They had all established themselves on the right side of the train. All the windows were open or broken out, and broken glass glistened on the coach floors.

"How long's it gonna' be?" one asked.

"When will we catch up to the bastards?" said another.

Selkirk shrugged. "Soon enough."

Selkirk picked his way through to the first coach. This coach was more crowded than the second, because everybody wanted to .get in their shots when the pursuit train pulled even. Nelsh's train wouldn't be expecting attack from another train. It would be ready for stationary ambush, a tree across the rails and gunmen beside the roadbed.

"When we pull level, stay down until it's time to fire," Selkirk ordered.

"I can see her smoke now!" one man shouted. "Stick your head way out the window. They can't be but three miles ahead."

The thundering of the mighty locomotives increased the sudden tension in the cars. Men checked their rifles for the umpteenth time, licked their lips, or took a couple of quick jolts of whiskey.

The pursuit train was making three miles for the other train's two and the target grew larger and larger, thundering across a river basin ahead.

"Ready. Everybody down."

With some complaint, the gunmen got down.

The brass railing of Nelsh's private car sparkled in the morning sun. Selkirk meant to concentrate fire on the flatcar. Kill Nelsh's army and the man himself would be easy prey.

The pursuit train threw the coal to her, picking up a few more miles per hour.

The locomotive was level with the rear platform

when the door opened and John Slocum stepped outside into the air, eyeing the cab of the overtaking train. He wore his plainsman's Stetson so it shaded his eyes and he carried a Winchester dangling loosely from his right hand. He lifted that hand in a casual wave.

One of the gunmen peeked. "I can pop that bastard," he said.

"No," Selkirk snapped. "Wait until we're broadside."

And, just as casually as he'd waved, John Slocum reversed his Winchester and blew the engineer right out of his cab. Selkirk saw the explosion, heard a scream, and saw something fall out of the train behind him. A second shot killed the fireman.

Slocum dove back inside the train as Welfleet's gunmen went to war.

The pursuit train was still behind Nelsh's train, though overtaking rapidly, and when the men jumped up in the car and began to fire, the near target was the rear of Jay Nelsh's private coach.

They poured a withering fire into the coach, pocking and ventilating the walls, destroying every window on the near side, blowing pieces out of the elaborate brass rail.

Both of Welfleet's cars were firing now, producing a murderous volley. A hundred bullets, two hundred, crashed through the car, and most of them bored right on through the far side.

Slocum, Nelsh, and the women were crouched behind Nelsh's great steel safe. The car was full of splinters and smoke and screaming bullets. The car shuddered and swayed as the bullets rocked it.

"Oh, my God!" Nelsh cried.

"Better they waste their bullets on us," Slocum said. "We'll get in our own licks soon enough."

Gradually the train advanced, a foot at a time. The gunmen leaned out of the windows in their eagerness, firing at the broken artifacts they could see through the shattered windows. Pots flew off the walls in the little kitchenette, and the oven door crashed open. Bullet after bullet crashed through Elizabeth Nelsh's open wardrobe door, as if the gunmen thought somebody might be hiding inside amidst the fancy dresses and cloaks.

Slocum had given explicit orders to the men in the flatcar. Let the senator's crew burn up their enthusiasm on the private car—then fire as one man. Protected by the timbered flatcar, they did just as they'd been told. They waited until the first coach was level with them before they rose up above their wooden bulwarks and fired a volley.

It was a terrible surprise. The gunmen were quite used to having it all their own way, and had become quite careless about exposing themselves. Ten of Welfleet's fifty died in that first volley.

It broke their fire. Men fell back inside the train, and a couple toppled out the windows. The flatcar managed another volley. Now the second coach was close enough to go into action and the fire was much more evenly applied, bullet for bullet, a slugfest of lead.

Men died on the flatcar; men died in the coach. Since there were so many more guns firing from Welfleet's cars, gradually the men in the flatcar sought cover. The bullets scored the wood above their angry heads and their own fire quit. Level with the boxcar, Welfleet's men continued to fire. They'd been stung once by surprise.

Nobody was inside but the horses. Suddenly hit, hurt and screaming horses jumped forward or back or against the sides of the car. After ten seconds of fire, thirty bullets in all, the gunmen stopped firing quite spontaneously.

One man spat. "I never hired on to kill good horses," he said—and he spoke for all of them.

But the damage had been done. Five animals were killed outright and twice that number hurt. And all of them panicked, lunging and squealing with pain.

Since the coaches were somewhat higher than the flatcars and since the fire was so fierce, none of Slocum's men dared to raise their heads for a shot.

Still pouring it on, the train passed by Nelsh's slower train, bullets ruining the steam valve and bell but not harming the engineer or fireman, who lay flat on the floor of the locomotive while the walls shook around them. The fireman touched the steel plate as a Sharps bullet hit, and the shock broke his hand.

The Indians watched the whole fight from the turret of the caboose. They enjoyed a good fight, but they didn't take an active part. It was a great pleasure to watch white men killing each other.

What could be shot off Nelsh's engine had been shot. There were scars on the boiler and broken windows in the cab. The water tank leaked a fine spray of spouted water from a dozen holes.

John Slocum climbed on top of Nelsh's shattered private car. Quite deliberately, he fired twice. The first slug dropped the engineer in the rear engine and the next took his fireman.

When Senator Welfleet pulled the signal cord in the prearranged signal—two short, one long—there was nobody alive to stop the train and reverse it, as had been his plan.

On it sped, faster now, with dead men in the cabs of both locomotives and the senator angrily tooting the whistle. A few men tried to fire at Slocum, but he'd popped down quickly and nobody really got a good shot at him.

When they saw the tender of the other train going by, Nelsh's engineer rose shakily to his feet. The din inside that steel cab had been frightening and continuous, and he thanked God he was alive. His hand had been cut by a glass fragment. He looked at the bright blood with real wonder.

Gently, the engineer cut the throttle just enough to let the pursuit train go by faster. Now that the murderous fire was lifted, the men in Slocum's flatcar fired at the rear of the other train, but they didn't do very much damage except to the paint work.

The pursuit train drew steadily away—a hundred yards, two hundred, three. Gently, Slocum's train throttled down. A fast horse could have caught it now, but it was still slowing.

Senator Welfleet knew perfectly well that something had gone wrong with his plan, and he yelled for somebody to do something about it. They were drawing away from Nelsh's train at such a rate that they'd soon be out of sight, and they weren't reversing. The second coach was full of triumphant men, untouched by that single volley. They'd shot the hell out of Nelsh's train as they inched by.

"Selkirk! Selkirk!" the senator cried.

The private secretary didn't hear his boss until

Nelsh's train was far behind them, out of sight around a bend. It took long minutes to get experienced trainmen forward to man the cab John Slocum had emptied and bring the train to a stop.

The senator took a drink from the common bottle as a sign of democratic instincts he didn't possess. He cried, "We'll reverse down this track and hit them again—and, by God, there'll be a bonus for every man jack on the train. Maybe they've stung us some," the senator said, "but, by God, we'll sting them to death!"

Slocum's train had halted where the roadbed crossed a shallow gully. The roadbed dropped into the gully here and he had twenty men lying along it, rifles ready. Their pride was hurt, but Welfleet's guns had only accounted for two dead and three wounded—and the horses, some still screaming in their locked boxcar.

There were some men who would have spent precious minutes turning the animals out of that car, but John Slocum wouldn't permit it.

"I want every man with loaded rifle and pistols," he said. "I want you to keep your ammunition ready to hand and to make your bullets count. Concentrate on the coaches. If you get a clean shot at a trainman, take it. They'll be coming back fast. When that train passes by, I don't want to see anything but smoke and lead."

Lena and Elizabeth worked at the very bottom of the gully. Lena wrapped bandages and Elizabeth was cleaning a wounded man's brow.

Nelsh chafed at being kept from the fight, but Slocum was insistent. "You start shooting, Nelsh, and I'll walk off this job. I'm here to keep you alive, and you ain't gonna make it harder for me."

A few men rolled smokes. Slocum lay back against the roadbed and looked at the sky. He'd be looking up at the sky when he died. Most men wanted to die in bed, surrounded by grieving friends and family. John Slocum hoped to die with his boots on, with the sky for a death canopy and vultures standing around like long-lost friends.

The sharp gravel under his back had been thrown by some laborer's shovel—how many months ago? And how long would it support the steel reality of Jay Nelsh's dream?

"She'll be coming soon," one man said. He had his ear to the track.

Slocum relaxed. The less he worked now, the more he'd do when he was needed. Nelsh looked awful damn unhappy sitting down at the bottom of the roadbed with the women. Lena's face was less harsh than it had been, and Elizabeth wasn't so prim. Life changes us all, Slocum thought.

Defiantly, the senator's new engineer sounded his steam whistle and, almost like an echo, the second locomotive followed suit.

Now they would hurtle down on the other train, firing into their midst, killing with repeated, lightning-fast attacks.

The driving wheels spun against the track and the mighty locomotives reversed, picking up speed, slowly, so slowly.

They expected to see Nelsh's train coming around the bend.

More speed now. The tumbleweed was starting to streak by. Senator Welfleet lit a cigar. Though he hadn't fired himself, he was as dirty as any of the other fighters, and he picked up a dead man's rifle. His blood was up, too.

The senator's train was doing fifty miles an hour as it rounded the bend. The gunmen were leaning out the windows again, trying to see past their own locomotive, looking for the other train. A cheer went up when they saw it.

On the roadbed, John Slocum poked his Sharps in front of him and drew a bead. He said quietly, "When I give the word, you fire, and keep on firing until they're past us. We'll hurt them this time, I expect."

The gunmen on the speeding train couldn't place their bullets with any accuracy. Their coach swung from side to side, throwing their sights off target before they could fire. Most of Slocum's men lay below grade level, with just their heads and their weapons visible.

A man clutched his heart and toppled out the window. An instant later they heard the boom of the rifle.

Now a patter of shots struck the speeding coach and another fighter drew back from the window with a curse, nursing his bloodied hand. "Oh, damn it. Oh, damn it all to hell."

A left-handed man had a better shot and didn't need to lean so far to get a shot off, but lefties weren't in great supply, and most of Welfleet's men started using their handguns. Maybe the distance was too great for effective shooting, but they didn't need to expose as much of themselves.

Selkirk figured it out before anyone else. Slocum's men were perfectly safe crouched below the grade, and their bullets would tell, while the men in the car were going to be inaccurate, exposed, and unarmored. Selkirk hurried back to the caboose.

Senator Welfleet judged the situation a moment later and took after him. Selkirk sat with his back to the plate.

Bullets were already punching through the sides of the caboose. The senator was awful to look at. Selkirk looked away. He didn't want to draw any attention to himself.

Welfleet's gunmen were frustrated. Whenever they leaned out for a shot, a hail of bullets drove them back inside. The new trainmen in the first locomotive were already dead.

Two pairs of brown legs descended the caboose ladder. The Apaches had bright black eyes. Quick slugs shattered the turret windows and glass cascaded down. One of the Apaches held a bow, the other carried a muzzle-loading cavalry carbine. It was short enough to be fired one-handed, and he held it like a big pistol. He looked from Welfleet to Selkirk. The two white men took up most of the steel plate.

The fire got hotter. A bullet bored through the wooden walls and out the other side. Men cried out in the coaches. The train continued to pick up speed.

For the first time the Apaches spoke in English. The one with the big carbine said "Go" to Selkirk.

"Go?"

The Apache gestured with his carbine. He wanted Selkirk to move over so he could be protected by the boiler plate.

Selkirk tried a tight smile. "Sorry, friend," he said. "Rank has its privileges."

The savage's carbine had a large ring hammer, and he drew it back with a heavy click.

Selkirk patted the floor at his feet. "Here," he suggested, "lie down here and you'll be quite safe."

Without changing expression, the Apache fired. The heavy slug passed through Selkirk's chest, killing him outright, and rang against the armor. When Selkirk toppled, the Apache leaned forward to examine the nick in the boiler plate, as interested in the dent as he was uninterested in the body at his feet.

There was room for two Indians and Senator Welfleet behind the steel plate. Just enough room. The Indians sat side by side, bracing their feet against Selkirk's body, silent and patient through the storm. Senator Welfleet made himself as small as he could.

The firing from Slocum's embankment was steady and though it didn't have the sheer ferocity of the broadsides from the pursuit train, it was thoughtful, deliberate, and very deadly.

Bullets punched into any man who dared show himself at the windows of the approaching train. Bullets punched through the thin walls, and inside was carnage, bodies rolling around underfoot, brave men weeping in terror.

The train continued to speed up and the cars rocked from side to side. Slocum's crew poured on the fire. The return fire was mostly wasted on the air or plunked into the abandoned cars of Nelsh's train

Most return fire had stopped when the pursuit train was a thousand yards up the track, but when Slocum's men slowed their fire, he was right at their elbows, urging more, still more. "We have them now, boys! Finish them!"

At close range the metal bounced to the steady

shocks and the wooden window frames simply disintegrated.

There were no unwounded men and most of the original crew was dead. The survivors lay behind body barricades, covered with the blood of their friends.

The senator's train finished its second and almost fatal pass. John Slocum was perfectly free to clamber onto his locomotive, where he fired two more rounds into the last locomotive of the pursuit train.

The train chuffed half a mile on down the track, slowing as the dying engineer put the last of his strength into stopping it.

Senator Welfleet's train had lost every skilled trainman on board. Down in the coaches there weren't half a dozen men still alive. Senator Welfleet stumbled through the cars toward the head of the train, his Indian allies with him, careless of where they stepped, indifferent to the blood. The cars looked like ill-designed colanders, with light glistening at each of two thousand bullet holes. No window was unbroken, no fixture unshattered. One Apache stepped on a wounded man and glanced down in surprise at the man's groan. No wounded Apache cries out.

Welfleet clambered forward. The lead locomotive was a better place to be, out in the open air. Down the track the senator could see Slocum's men shouting and cheering. Unmindful of discipline, they capered around on the track like a bunch of wild baboons.

The sight of their joy straightened him out. The Apache gestured at the unfamiliar controls of the locomotive. "Go," he said.

"Now there's an idea."

The savage understood the mockery in the tone and leveled the carbine at the senator's chest. Contemptuously, Senator Welfleet pushed it away. "You'll find it hard to 'go' without me" he snapped.

He identified the throttle. He supposed the great lever on the floor was either the hand brake or the gears. Unceremoniously, the Indians hurled the dead trainmen off the train.

Slocum's men knew the terrible damage they had inflicted. They knew the fight was over. Some of them had already broken out whiskey bottles, which flew hand to hand faster than the laughter and cheering.

Jay Nelsh stood on the tracks, shaking his head. "God," he said. "Oh, God."

John Slocum nodded at him as one human being to another, two men caught in the horror.

Though everybody saw Senator Welfleet's train pulling near, nobody could credit it. Smoke poured from the lead locomotive, growing larger in everyone's eyes.

"Christ! Here they come again!"

It made the fighters furious. They had defeated the enemy. They had slaughtered until they were tired of slaughter. Now the enemy was coming back again.

One or two shook their fists. One or two cursed. Most men simply returned to their positions along the embankment, grimly determined to do their duty

They loaded their weapons and listened to Slocum's instructions. "I don't know what these jaspers are up to, but they must have some poison still in them. It's up to us to pull their fangs. The first volley when the coach draws level. Then fire at will."

John Slocum was fixing a bundle of dynamite—

ten sticks of the stuff. The fuse was inserted and crimped. He didn't have time to time the unfamiliar fuse, but he figured it'd burn at the rate of one second per inch, which was standard. With the bundle in his right hand, he lay down in the steel cab of his locomotive. If he couldn't shoot the other train off the tracks, by God, he'd blow it off.

Senator Welfleet sat between his allies, the firebox full, the throttle wide open. Here he should be safe from the bullets. His allies smelled awful. The floor of the cab was smeared with blood. He still had one card to play—the card he hadn't wished to play at all. It was hot, god-awful hot, and the steam pressure built to a fury in the Pacific's boiler. Nothing to do but wait.

A hundred yards, fifty, twenty-five . . . The restless fighters put their weapons to their shoulders. Their broadside wasn't quite perfect, but it did more damage. Their withering fire killed the last men in the coaches, and the shock of all those bullets nearly threw the train off the tracks. Bullets tore through the passenger cars and Welfleet's armored caboose. Bullets sought them in the cab of the locomotive. There was no return fire, not a round. The train they fought was a ghost train.

Slocum tossed his sparking package through the air. The dynamite flew through the window in the turret of the caboose and vanished in the bowels of the car. Slocum covered his ears, counting.

Except for the shattered windows and the shot-away window frames, the pursuit train looked like any other train. The boilers of both tenders leaked water.

Senator Welfleet had both hands over his ears,

weeping like a child. The firing dwindled, dwindled, and then the entire train rocked again. The charge blew the sides right out of the caboose, lifting it right off its forward trucks. For an instant the train pulled the wreck, but then it uncoupled itself, and slowly the remains of the caboose and the rear locomotive derailed. Slocum's men cheered at the destruction, and even Jay Nelsh cheered, though the engine that lay like some dead pachyderm was one of his own.

The ruined train limped away. Slocum got a fine cheer, led by Jay Nelsh and old Jake. Elizabeth Nelsh stood on her tiptoes and gave Slocum a quick little kiss on the lips, and everyone cheered the kiss.

Welfleet's train was miles down the track before the man dared to get up. The Apaches in the cab laughed at him. If he had been an Apache, they would have killed him for showing fear.

The two Indians wouldn't help with the train, so the senator filled the roaring firebox, scraping coal until the blisters came and he thought his back would break. The train gradually slowed because he wasn't quite quick enough and didn't know how to conserve his steam.

Sweating, coal-blackened, as weary as he'd ever been in his life, Senator Welfleet kept the train rolling twenty miles east, very near to the halfway point between Gull and end of track.

The work train that had slipped out the night before waited there. Geronimo's men had toppled their locomotive across both tracks, ruining them completely. Since the train was ruined, the Apaches had staked the engine crew out and played with them with their knives. None of the white men had died well.

Senator Welfleet stumbled down from his locomotive to face the mocking eyes of his only remaining ally, Geronimo. Geronimo made a great circle with his right arm, indicating the great distance, the three staked-out whites, and the ruined tracks. "Here," he said.

Slocum's men sprawled, exhausted. They were too weary even to get drunk. Slocum had work to do with the horses. He killed the worst hurt and laid their bodies beside the track. When he was done, he had five sound animals left.

It was supper time before they finished but nobody had much of an appetite. Everybody wanted to be elsewhere. The crew longed for Gull or Fargo and Jay Nelsh meant to get back to Chicago as quickly as he could. Lena figured she'd ride as far east as they'd let her. No matter how tough it was in Chicago, it had to be easier than here. John Slocum was feeling the great weariness that comes on a man after he's done his very best at top speed for hours. The three hours of actual fighting had seemed like as many days.

The inside of Nelsh's car was pretty depressing and the flatcar was full of exhausted gunmen, so Slocum perched himself on top of the tender, his back against a pile of coal, and closed his eyes. Just fifteen minutes . . .

He woke when a cool hand touched his face.

"Hello, Elizabeth." He stretched. "Where are we?"

"Almost halfway," she said. "Are you feeling all right?"

"Yeah. I just needed a little shut-eye."

"Most of the men are the same. Oh, there are a few drinking and bragging, but not many."

"Your father?"

"He and Jake are trying to sort out his papers and documents. His office was shot up pretty bad."

"Uh-huh."

"This hasn't changed anything. He still has track to lay."

A honking triangle of geese flew by overhead. They were so beautiful they made Slocum's heart sad. "He'll need good luck," he said shortly.

She let her eyes roam over his face. "John, what do you want out of life?"

He thought about making a flippant reply, but she meant her question so he gave it some thought. "Freedom," he said finally.

"Just that?"

"Yep."

"I always hoped I'd . . . I'd be of use to somebody some time."

"Somebody's wife? Somebody's mother?"

"I suppose so. You make those jobs sound small and unimportant, but everybody can't be a great railroad builder, and everybody can't be free."

"I came out here in Sixty-six. Did I ever tell you that?" said Slocum.

"No."

Slocum thought about how it had been then, how much space, how many buffalo, how the tall prairie grass waved, and the chance of placer gold lay in every new stream. "Long time ago," he said.

She asked, "Will we have more trouble?"

"Depends if Welfleet's still kickin'. If he's got legs to stand on, he has to make another try. If we get back to Fargo with our story, his day is done."

"What kind of attempt?" She looked worried again.

"You keep askin' me questions I suppose I should know the answers to," he said.

She searched his face for a very long time and felt a twinge in her heart. "I've never met a man like you," she admitted.

There wasn't anything to say to that, so he said nothing.

"The men I've met have been gentlemen," she went on.

"Like Newell?"

"Precisely. Good dancers, well mannered, sweet-smelling . . ."

"Ambitious?"

"That, too." She sighed. "You wouldn't like to marry me, Mr. Slocum, would you?"

Caught by surprise, Slocum's face crinkled. "What on earth for?"

Her laughter was quite gay. "Then that's settled. Because I would not marry you either. The prospect of your face across the breakfast table in our Chicago home is terrifying. But perhaps we could try something else."

Slocum shook his head in disbelief. "Sure," he said.

She took his big hand in her little one and held it as the train hurried eastward.

The wind was getting chillier and Slocum could feel the first bite of the winter in the air.

Her hand was as light as duck down on his own. The country was getting rougher; there were some curves in the track. Here some glacier had left deposits of terminal moraine as it withdrew sullenly north, ten thousand years ago. The moraines held water better than the surrounding ground and were slightly greener, too.

Slocum pulled his hand from hers and stood up. "I want you to go back and tell the men to be on the alert," he said. "Tell them to see to their weapons."

"Why? What's wrong?"

"If I was Welfleet, I'd be thinking about an ambush. And this is awful good country for it."

He scrambled forward to the locomotive cab.

"Throttle back," he said. "Watch for trouble on the track."

The engineer stuck his head out and the train slowed. The fireman slung scoops of coal into the firebox and the train clattered at the track joints. They traveled one turn after another with no more trouble than a few tumbleweeds blowing against the cowcatcher.

"Up ahead," the engineer called, and a moment later Slocum saw it; Welfleet's shot-up train.

The engineer grabbed for the gear lever and Slocum tugged the steam whistle, three sharp toots to alert his men.

A sad trickle of smoke still rose from Welfleet's stack. No other sign of life. Slocum jerked the steam cord again, a long whistle.

Welfleet's train was abandoned, empty. Far off, perhaps five miles, Slocum could see a lone red butte like an ocean liner above the plain. He heard his own breathing.

"Jesus," the engineer said. He jerked the gear lever into full reverse. Geronimo's locomotive was crashed across both tracks blocking them.

John Slocum threw his rifle to his shoulder but he

couldn't see anything. Anything living, anyway. Plenty of corpses were inside Welfleet's destroyed train.

"Get us out of here," Slocum snapped.

The engineer's hand went to the throttle again, hesitated, and reached up to pick at the feathered shaft that had quite pierced his throat. He tried to say something, and it was probably important, but he couldn't manage. He took one step and, like a man taking a stroll on air, he walked out of the cab. Slocum dropped as another arrow banged into the steel. "Oh, hell," he said, and grabbed the throttle himself.

A flight of arrows plucked at the men on the flatcar and dropped several. The men replied with gunfire, shooting the hell out of the emptiness. The train withdrew, backing furiously. Slocum peered around the back edge of the cab, mad as hell, looking for something to shoot. He wished they'd used rifles. Rifles would leave smoke. His finger tightened on the trigger, but damned if he'd loose off a round out of pure nervousness.

In a few moments they were out of arrowshot and the train huffed backward. A few moments later Slocum's men ceased their ineffectual fire.

"They got Jim, damn their eyes!"

"Red Smith is dead, too. Arrow clean through him."

Slocum asked the fireman if he could handle the train by himself and he said he sure could.

The damage wasn't too awful—five dead, including the engineer, and another six not too badly wounded. Slocum didn't worry about them until Lena cried out, "John, he's turning blue!"

Indeed the man was. Not bright blue, more a

lavender blue, and his breath was coming in short gasps. He was dying though the arrow had lodged in his collarbone, hardly a fatal wound.

"They're poisoned. Don't handle the arrowheads," Slocum said.

While men gathered the shafts and hurled them from the train, the wounded men watched one another for the first signs. The signs weren't slow in coming. One after the other, the wounded men went into convulsions and died. It made everybody afraid, and it made them mad, too, because they didn't like feeling afraid. They thought the poisoned arrows were a particularly cowardly trick.

Slocum counted his men. Thirteen, if he counted Jay Nelsh, old Jake, and the fireman, who was hollering something now and pointing. The driving wheels squealed and complained once more.

The rails were gone behind them.

"They move fast," Slocum said.

The train came to a dead stop. The wind carried the cinders forward for a change. Men hunched low behind the wooden bulwarks of the cars.

Two sections of destroyed rails—the train couldn't go forward or back. The empty plain stretched out on both sides and nothing—absolutely nothing—moved. Slocum shivered. A man fired suddenly and the noise made them all jump. Slocum saw where his bullet hit, tossing a great gout of dirt in the air.

"I thought I saw something," the man mumbled by way of apology.

Slocum sat with his back to the wooden ties, trying to figure it. The Apaches had the train immobilized and, if Slocum was any judge, they'd have the telegraph cut too. No more locomotives at end of track and no way of summoning a rescue train anyway. No telling how long they'd be here before another train came poking west from Fargo.

He crept back to the private car, exposing himself as little as possible. between the cars. Inside the wrecked car, Elizabeth helped her father with his ruined papers while old Jake prowled from one window to another. Jake's rifle was ready.

The armchair Slocum sat in was springs, torn cowhide, and ripped horsehair. He sat carefully.

"You ever fight 'pache?" he asked Jake.

"Once. Outside of Yuma. Three of them rode up on the stage I was driving. We killed one. They killed the man riding shotgun."

"They fight at night?"

Few of the plains Indians fought in the darkness. They feared that their souls, if slain, couldn't find their way into the shadowland and would wander forever as ghosts. Blackfeet, Crows, and Sioux hated night fighting. Comanches weren't quite so particular.

"Hell, I don't know if they do or not."

A scream came from the flatcar. Jake and John Slocum were at the windows. Nothing moved. Slocum went forward to shout his question.

"It was Drafty Bob. He stood up to take a piss. He ain't dead, but he will be soon."

"Stay down! Stay down! They ain't gonna hit you if you keep your heads low."

"They'll likely rush us after a while," Jake said quietly.

"Likely they will. I wonder how many of our boys have ever been through it?"

It was Jake's turn to shrug. "What are you gonna do?"

"We got five good horses. Man with a good horse could get to help in three, four hours if he didn't spare the animal."

"Might get killed."

Jay Nelsh listened to the conversation with growing horror. He was not a frightened man. He was a childish man and, when the bullets started to fly, he had no thought beyond salvaging what he could of his charts and maps. He could conceive of his railroad failing, because his railroad was his whole life. He couldn't conceive of himself dying, because he never thought about his life apart from his work.

If he died, the railroad would fail. That was the inescapable keystone of Senator Welfleet's plan. Finally, Jay Nelsh feared it would work.

The bullets that roamed around him this morning seeking flesh behind the steel were impersonal. So long as the train was moving, Jay Nelsh didn't worry. The ruined car, the shattered portraits, maps, and charts didn't upset him. Now they were stopped. Stopped dead. "Slocum," he said, "you'll have to get us out of this."

"I'm doin' my best."

"If I'm killed, the railroad will go into bankruptcy."

"Father, I'll likely be killed, too."

"Nonsense. Welfleet is a competitor, not a monster."

"I think things might have got a little out of hand," Slocum said quietly. "Jake, will you chance it?"

The old man sighed. "It ain't much of a chance."

"No. But I seen you ride a couple of times."

"That was years ago, John."

"No hard feelings, then." Slocum turned away.

The old man exploded, "Jesus, John! I never said I wouldn't do it!"

Slocum said he'd get Jake to the boxcar and work out some sort of diversion. "They might be all day slipping up on us. I don't know how close they are but no Apache arrow will kill a man more than two hundred yards away. You better figure they're pretty close."

"I wish I could see 'em."

"You bet." Slocum clapped the older man on the arm. He found Jay Nelsh a pistol. Nelsh objected. "If you can't bear to kill Apaches, just put the gun to your temple, cock the hammer, and pull the trigger. It'll do the job faster than they will."

The horses were pretty spooky. Slocum wanted Jake to have two horses; one for a spare. "We don't even know if they got mounts out there," Slocum reminded him. "We sure know they can ride."

"Naw, I hate ridin' with another horse right behind me. I'll chance it with the one."

"Good luck."

The old man smiled. "I expect I'll need it." Jake's hands were trembling on the reins.

At Slocum's command, the men in the flatcar would open a withering fire, concentrating at any bush or shrub big enough to conceal a man.

"Now!"

With a roar the rifles spoke, spoke, spoke again. They announced danger and death. They made the earth toss and heave. Old Jake jumped his horse out of the car, lashing the hell out of his mount. The horse settled down quick, which was a piece of good luck, since the horse didn't know Jack from Adam.

A hundred yards—two hundred. It was no more

than a flicker, the sun touching the shaft of the arrow, but Slocum backtracked the shaft and put one, two, three into some low greasewood and, by God, a man stood up in that greasewood and gave his death cry and toppled forward where everybody could see him.

It was the first Apache they'd seen.

His arrow had done its work. Only the feathers were visible behind the horse's front shoulder. The horse ran another two hundred yards full tilt before its lungs filled and it drowned in its own blood.

The horses's front legs crumpled and old Jake kicked out of the stirrups and went over the horse's head. In front of him were hundreds of miles of nothing—behind him a band of Apaches. Jake didn't have any trouble deciding which direction held the greatest promise. He didn't even slow down, just kept running toward the far horizon.

"Goddamn," Slocum cursed, and snapped around at a shadow that went after the old man.

Jake vanished behind a low rise and Slocum tried another shot at something—looked like smoke—that followed him.

Jake didn't reappear. After the thunder of the guns, the silence was brittle and nervous. The Indian Slocum had killed lay where he had fallen. Others put a few bullets into his body, scared of the man even though he was dead.

Slocum sat down. Lena came forward and sat beside him. "Will he get away?"

"I've heard it said an Apache brave can outrun a horse. Takes him two, three days to bring it down, but they generally get the horses they start after." Slocum was hoping for a single shot. Just one. One bullet that meant they hadn't taken the old man alive. "Maybe you could scare up some grub. I don't know when they'll come at us, and I'd sooner die with a full belly."

"You know how to give a girl hope."

"We can hope for the cavalry, but I hear they're a couple hundred miles west of here."

In half an hour Lena was back with some slices of beef and dry biscuits left over from breakfast. The food tasted like sawdust in Slocum's mouth. Most of the men wouldn't eat anything at all.

The fireman was touched by an arrow as he scrambled across the tender toward the flatcar seeking the safety numbers provided but he was very lucky. The poisoned arrow pinned part of his loose sleeve, but the deadly tip didn't break his flesh. When he landed in the car and hurled the arrow over the side, he had a gray face.

Slocum said, "I'll bet you didn't sign up for this when you decided to be a railroad man."

The fireman snarled. "You damn right! You damn right!" Some of the color returned to his face.

The sky overhead was indifferent, and there was no protection from the colorless sun.

They were pretty low on provisions. Two days' food, perhaps half of it shot up and ruined. Only a few gallons of water hadn't been spilled in the bullet storm. Not enough for the humans let alone the horses.

Slocum had eight men to repel the attack when it came. They had plenty of ammunition, but they were pretty well pinned down. If night fell before the Apaches made their attack, they'd try to dig some rifle pits beside the track, but they'd need the darkness for that.

Slocum repositioned his men so they spread over the whole train. Nobody wanted to go. They felt safer in the flatcar. But Slocum couldn't afford to have any part of the train unguarded.

Two, three, and two—that's how he lined them up. He left Nelsh with the women and roamed all the cars himself.

Near three o'clock he spotted one. No gross movement gave the Indian away. He was completely behind a mesquite bush with none of his body showing. But Slocum noted something wrong with the shadows in that particular mesquite, some unexplained darkness. He slumped behind the timbers and waited for a full ten minutes before he popped his head up again at the opposite end of the car.

That particular mesquite bush wasn't seventy-five feet from the train and if the shape he'd seen really was an Apache, the Indians were too damn close. He wondered how many Indians Welfleet had. He had no illusions as to who was commanding them. That Indian face peering through the ripped tent at end of track could only have been one man—Geronimo.

Twenty minutes later he scurried across the locomotive tender, low and fast. The two men in the cab were glad to see him.

"Hot up here, ain't it?" Slocum remarked.

"Yeah. Well, the firebox is dying out." The man slammed his fist into the control panel. "I sure wish we had some track."

"I expect that'd be all right," Slocum said, slowly and judiciously. He hoped to provoke a grin, without success. These men were serious—seriously afraid.

"I'm gonna try a shot with this Sharps here. I want you to hoot the hell out of the whistle and then I'll likely shoot. They may come at us then. You ready?"

The two men saw to their weapons. One stationed himself beside the whistle pull; the other got ready to back Slocum's play.

The steam whistle shrieked. Slocum was expecting the sound and he flinched. The Indian, who wasn't expecting the sudden noise, flinched too— and John Slocum touched one off. The heavy rifle slammed back into his shoulder and the peppery smell of new-fired black powder filled the air. The heavy slug didn't kill the Apache behind the bush, but it ruined his right shoulder and shoved him into the open.

That was all it took. The man bared his teeth and jumped to his feet, and he was dead in the air.

The angry guns of the defenders slapped into his head and chest. Usually a dead man will fall forward. This Apache sat down and flopped onto his back, punched over by slugs.

The defenders raised a jagged cheer. Slocum waited for the attack.

It didn't come.

The sun moved west. Slocum slipped from one car to another. The Indians didn't try an arrow. They were too close to risk an arrow. His eyes moved constantly across the plains, seeking displacement. He never stared; he let his peripheral vision work for him.

He talked to his men, told awkward stories, and urged them to keep a special watch to the northwest because that was where the Indians would likely come. He urged them to keep their wits about them, because the Apaches were tricky devils.

Jay Nelsh had quit on his ruined files and was cleaning up the little kitchen as best he could. He'd salvaged a small bowl of broken eggs and half a ham. He'd broken strips of carving off the walls to fuel the wood stove and had a pretty good fire going.

"They'll be on us momentarily," Slocum said.

Nelsh nodded and went back to making his work area useful. "I never once fired a gun, you know," he said. "Never enjoyed hunting—never liked the damn things. Oh," he stopped, "they're beautiful machines, I give you that."

John Slocum looked at his Colt—greasy with his sweat, stained at the muzzle and cylinder from the explosions. It looked like a dirty tool. "They won't attack with arrows. They've got repeating rifles."

"Then Lena's bandages will be of use. I intend to heat up this ham and, once I pick the shells out of the eggs, I can make scrambled eggs to go with it." He held up a jar. It looked like it was full of buckshot.

"Caviar," Nelsh explained. "Beluga caviar. The bullets missed it, and it'll be just great on the eggs."

Slocum smiled at the man's smile. He thought Jay Nelsh was quite mad, but lucky, too.

Vigilance is tiring. Slocum's men took turns—one watched, one slept—as the afternoon dwindled on.

It was a big event when another flock of birds went over, too high this time to tell if they were ducks or geese. The buzzards were circling Welfleet's train, getting up courage.

Lena and Elizabeth tore bandages, squares, and strips from the fresh ruined sheets in the private car's linen chest. Elizabeth worked better than Lena did, which was a fact Lena resented because she thought of Elizabeth as useless for anything but marriage and formal parties.

Lena thought this kind of work was beneath her. She'd gone into whoring because she didn't care to do housework for any man, and this was suspiciously like housework.

"How many of these damn things we have to make?" She gestured at the pile beside them.

"Do you have anything better to do?" Elizabeth asked. She'd had to nudge and push Lena all afternoon to get a little work from her. The two women were not destined to be friends.

The girls spent the long afternoon quarrelling over the bandages, quarrelling over the arrangements they made for the wounded. Low-grade quarrels—one way unhappy people pass the time.

Jay Nelsh fed the men himself, taking the few surviving plates out to them, washing them, filling them again. Most of the men ate the ham and scrambled eggs, and one or two tried the caviar.

The Apaches came at the perfect time. The sun was sinking in the horizon and the earth on their side of it was quite black. Blackness and glare. If a man shaded his eyes, he could almost see in that direction, could almost see running figures. "Hey!" the fireman shouted, and a bullet knocked him in the head for his trouble.

Slocum opened fire with his handgun. Jesus, they were close—jumping from the earth—the nearest one not more than forty feet from the roadbed. Fired, tagged one. Fired, maybe wounded another.

The Indians were shooting, too. Not awful accurate,

but they were close enough so they didn't have to be.

An Apache clambered along the top of the locomotive and swung into the cab, swinging with a long, broad-bladed skinning knife. One man went down with a slash across the belly. The other grabbed the Indian's hand and screamed for help.

An Indian kicked open the back door of the private car. Big Indian with a lever-action rifle, eyes darting this way and that, rifle darting too, telegraphing his intention to shoot.

He saw two men, the women, and an unarmed white man in a chef's apron.

Lena picked up her pistol and fired. Though the Apache's trigger finger jerked, he didn't shoot anything in that car that hadn't been shot before. Lena looked at the pistol in her hand and started to cry. Still crying, she stepped to the ruined door, trying to force it shut. A bullet sent her down. "Oh!" she said. The blood splotched her breast. "I'll be the first customer for our bandages, Elizabeth," she said quite perkily. A bubble of blood came to her mouth. She swallowed some blood, swallowed some more, then died.

Another defender crushed the skull of the Indian wrestling in the cab. Bullets rang into the heavy ties, but nobody else was rushing the train. Slocum poured his bullets into the muzzle blasts of the Indians, firing as fast as he could, spreading his shots. He was sure he hit one, maybe two, but he never got a clear glimpse of his kills.

The last shot. The smoke hung over the plain for a moment before it dispersed. After a bit, a night bird called nervously. Damn dumb thing.

"Sing out!" Slocum said. "How many we got left to fight?"

The defenders watching both sides of the train called out their names. Five of them, including the man in the locomotive, not counting Nelsh. Nelsh and Elizabeth laid Lena out on the beautiful oriental carpet, where her blood was brighter and would be blacker than the rug's most vivid hue.

"This is terrible," Nelsh said.

Slocum ignored the man. "Elizabeth," he said quietly, "there's nothing you can do for her. And we've got wounded in the flatcar." The wounded had only flesh wounds, but Slocum wanted to keep the girl occupied.

After the sun was gone, the sky stayed light over the dark earth for a long time. A few clouds drifted by overhead. Somewhere, far in the West, the sun was still shining. Slocum wished he was there.

Five men, himself, Elizabeth, and Nelsh. No telling how many Apaches. Couldn't be a tremendous number or they would have taken the train in their first assault. He wished he could light up a quirly. "I don't want any smoking!" he called out. "If you need tobacco, chew it. Anyone who shows a light, if the Apaches don't get him, I will." He put tobacco quite out of his mind.

When would they hit again? Would they wait until that still, sad hour just before dawn, when men are so close to the grave? "Mr. Nelsh, I'm going to have to use you on guard. I'll put you into the locomotive and a second man on top of the boxcar. The height should help us see better."

"Of course," Nelsh said. "Of course." Then he

added, "It could have been Elizabeth closing that door instead of the other girl. My Elizabeth."

"It could."

"John." The man was quite serious. His lips were firm, his eyes strong. "What's one man's life worth?"

Slocum shook his head. He thought of saying, "A man's life is worth how many other men will die for him." But Nelsh was gone by then.

Slocum waited for the moon to come up. It seemed like a long wait, and it was black as the inside of a cat before its first pale glow showed itself, chasing long shadows across the desolate plain.

Plenty of stars, and the Milky Way was quite brilliant. A shooting star. Another. Elizabeth took her place beside him.

"So many shooting stars. I used to wish on them when I was a girl."

"I hope you're wishing on them now."

"I've prayed."

"Good. No harm in that," he said.

"Will we be alive tomorrow night, John?"

No sound anywhere along the train. The man on the boxcar was awake and, hopefully, Jay Nelsh, up front in the locomotive. The earth was silver between the brushy patches. Silver, gray, and black. "Sure," he lied.

"I have my room cleaned up," she said.

"Uh-huh."

"It isn't perfect, but it's much better." She paused. "There's a bed."

'It was his turn to pause. "All right," he said, finally.

"Thanks for your eagerness," she said over her shoulder.

He followed her with rifle slung over his shoulder. "I never have been over fond of virgins," he said.

"I thought a woman's virginity was her finest jewel," she retorted. "At least Captain Newell thought so."

"Yeah. He was about half right."

She stood in front of the door to her compartment. Boldly she slid the steel door open. All the glass on that side of the train was gone, but she'd swept it out. Big, open square of a window framed by a couple of irregular curtains—torn dresses she'd put up.

The bed was a simple white rectangle. "I stretched a couple of blankets over the mattress to hold the stuffing," she explained, proud as any homemaker. She patted the sheet that covered her handiwork and retreated clumsily, mightily embarrassed.

Slocum rested his rifle against the wall and sat down on the bed. "Sit down, Elizabeth," he said quietly.

She sat, almost close to him, almost far away. The air hummed with her nervousness. "You were the first person to call me Elizabeth," she said.

"Uh-huh."

"Have you had very many girls—women, I mean?"

"Several."

"Well, I went with Captain Newell to his hotel. In Chicago, I mean. It hurt me, and afterwards he was afraid I'd tell my father. Not," she added, "that father would have cared."

"He cares about you," he said. "That's what's got him up on the engine with a rifle in his hand— his caring for you."

She wore a bright blouse and a white dress with

flounces that looked like a Navajo Indian dress. She wore an emerald necklace around her throat. She leaned over, still clumsy, and set her lips on his.

He didn't want her. His mind was on the Indians, on tomorrow, on death.

Her lips were very soft and slightly moist and as gentle as a child's. She scooted over to him and pressed harder, lips demanding now, demanding her share.

He broke away. "Elizabeth . . ."

Her face flickered between hurt and stubborn pride. It settled on pride. "John Slocum, if I must die, I would much rather die as a woman." She tugged, and the torn dresses rustled as they covered most of the window.

Just a little light. A little light to see her upper body, proud of her body, proud of her breasts. Breasts which probably would never suckle children.

She didn't cover herself, but she let him have an eyeful. And, despite himself, his cold body warmed; the blood flowed back into his chilly hands. "Yes," he said.

He was filthy dirty, covered with soot and gunpowder. She wasn't much cleaner. The poor light disguised that fact and she was a blur to him, a blur of hues, shadowed browns, shadowed grays. Her triangle was as dark as the hair on her head. And the hollows of her: hollows on the backs of her arms, hollows behind her knees, hollows below her skull, a hollow in the center of her throat.

He touched her there.

She was shyer than he. When he was naked, she touched the scar under his rib cage where that half-breed had planted his boot knife. Her hands traced

the strong muscles of his shoulders and his back,
under the shoulder blades, across the ridged scars
where he'd been flogged so many years ago. She
touched those scars like they were all she needed to
know of him, and perhaps she was correct.

"John? Hold me very tightly, or I'll be afriad."

So he pressed her close, not as hard as he might
have, but hard enough so she'd feel his strength.

She went back to touching him, his lips, his eyes,
his chest. She giggled when she dipped her finger
into his navel.

He stroked her smooth breasts and felt the life
awaken in the tips of them.

This one would die tomorrow? Never to know her
own home, her own babies?

Slocum thought he would die first.

She tugged at his pubic hair and he felt rather than
saw her smile in the dark. He could smell her now,
the rich female musk. She held him in her hand,
wondering. "John . . ."

He lay back then and swung his heels up on the
bed. Flat on his back, hands under his head.

"John . . . ?"

She released him and slid up on his body, her
breasts pressing against his chest, her legs clamping
his, her body hair brushing his. She buried her head
in his shoulder.

Outside a hoot owl called its soft coo. Her heart
beat against his and her breath was on his neck, and
he wondered how it could be that a hundred-pound
woman could lie so light on his chest the way she
did.

The world is full of dangers outside your woman's

arms. Slocum held her behind her little rump, her soft pubic hair on his belly.

Her lips found his again and they were no girl's lips, but a woman's with all a woman's ferocity, all her needs. She wanted—oh, how she wanted! Arms around her shoulders, her own hands working furiously between their bodies.

"Hey," he chuckled, "you ain't gonna get it in that way."

"John?" Half anger, half plea.

"Either you get underneath me, or else you get up straight and kind of slide it in that way."

"I don't want to be underneath. I never want to be underneath any more."

"Then you're gonna do all the work. Just get back a little, lean up now."

Their hands met on his cock. "Don't tug it off," he said.

She turned loose once he was wedged an inch or so, just deeper than the furrow itself.

She grunted. She rested her weight on her hands. Her breasts were taut above him. "Now what?" she asked.

"Didn't Newell show you anything?"

"He taught me how men and women breed," she snapped, unhappy to be reminded. She was being new and fresh for him, and if he couldn't appreciate that—

"Just be still. Be as still as you can."

It was like he was spreading her apart, like she had something caught in her belly, like she was melting. She licked her lips. "Oh," she said, "John . . ."

"You sure like to talk a lot."

"John, I can feel it in me. Oh, John . . ." She tried a little experimental bounce and she slid down and gasped, until their hair intertwined.

He began an easy motion then, working her, milking her depths, letting her know.

She leaned forward until her breasts were thumping against his chest and her back rose and fell. She slapped against his legs with her butt and found his mouth again.

She moved quicker and forgot about his mouth and went for her own pleasure, seeking she didn't know what.

She found it with little cries, and he hadn't meant to come, but she took that decision from him.

When she slumped, sweaty belly to sweaty belly, he reached where he'd discarded his clothes and covered her with his smelly old shirt.

After a while he slipped out.

"Why'd you do that?" She reached down and tried to put him back in, but it was no use. "Where'd you go? I liked you in there."

"Uh-huh. If you keep wigglin' around you're gonna toss the shirt on the floor again."

"How can I get you back inside of me?"

He told her. She was surprised that her mouth could do that much good, but was willing to give anything a try. She coughed once and had a little trouble scraping him with her teeth but it wasn't awfully long before she had her wish.

They had each other again. Not so long this time, but no less tender. Near the end he grabbed her and jammed his seed as far into her as it was meant to go. Her face wore a look of beatific surprise and when she bent to kiss him, he could taste himself on her breath.

"Can you lie with me here, John?"

He was warm and weary. "I got to see to the sentries," he said. "If the bastards surprise us, we'll be in an awful fix."

She grinned at him. Her teeth shone. "If they kill me right now," she said, "I couldn't be happier."

The crazy stars careening overhead were no crazier than John Slocum's mind. It's always easier to fight when you don't really care for anything past the fight itself. A man who fights for what he loves is handicapped by that love. A man protecting a lover can be killed, and the lover becomes fair prey.

Slocum sat with the guard on the boxcar for a while. He hadn't seen anything. Some shadows he thought were Apaches but turned out to be shadows. He wouldn't shoot unless he had an Indian at the end of his sights, no, sir.

Slocum patted his shoulder. "Good. You just keep your eyes open."

"Mr. Slocum?"

Slocum peered a little closer. Just a kid, not more than eighteen or nineteen years old. He was doing fine for his first big fight.

"Yeah?"

"You don't have to answer this, Mr. Slocum, but seein' as how . . ." The kid waved at the empty dangerous plains. "I had a pal once who told me you rode with Quantrill's guerrillas during the war. I said you never, and I bet a silver dollar on it. Would you tell me the right of the matter?"

"You owe your pard a dollar, son. Keep a sharp eye." Slocum slipped back down the way he'd come.

Three men asleep in the flatcar, curled under their coats. Every man kept one hand on his rifle. One man looked to be sleeping on top of his. That'd make a hard bed.

Jay Nelsh sat on the cab of his locomotive with his legs crossed like the Buddhas a man can see in San Francisco's Chinatown.

"I'll take a watch," Slocum said. "Go ahead and get some sleep."

The pale light made Nelsh's profile stark as the surface of the moon. "No, thanks, I couldn't. I'll stay up."

"Suit yourself." Nelsh's rifle lay on the flat roof with the lever drawn. Slocum completed the job of levering a round into the chamber. He released the hammer gently. "The first shot, just cock the hammer and let fly. You have to use the lever for the other bullets. When you run out of bullets, either reload, or use the damn thing as a club."

"You don't think very much of me, do you, Slocum?"

"You? To tell the truth, I hadn't thought much about it."

"What will the Apaches do if they capture Elizabeth?"

"They won't capture Elizabeth." Slocum was very sure of that.

"You'd . . . ? I see."

"There's plenty of things worse than death, Nelsh."

"I suppose so. Mr. Slocum, would you tell me about the Apache?"

"Ain't much to tell. I never fought 'em before. All I can go on is what I hear. Everybody makes the fighting tribes to be fifteen times worse than they are, because that way the army is quick to send troops. Tell the truth about them and the troops go where the other settlers are lying. I heard the Apaches are tougher than whang leather and twice as mean. I heard they're crazy. Once heard it isn't uncommon for an Apache brave to turn to the next man in a file and kill him, quick as that, for no cause whatsoever. We hunt the Apache. The Mexican army hunts the Apache. They ain't got no particular friends in the world. I guess that'd be bound to make you a little crazy.''

"Do they have a code of honor?''

Slocum's face wore its puzzlement openly. "Of course they got a code of honor. Hell,'' he smiled, "the more pushed and hurt and battered an Indian is, the bigger his code of honor. Oh, the Apache are honorable all right. They got nothin' else but their honor.''

Slocum prowled the cars for another hour or so. When he figured it was three A.M., he woke two men to relieve his sentries. The kid on the boxcar came down gratefully enough, but Nelsh said he could handle it.

"Suit yourself.'' None of Slocum's business if the man wanted to be a martyr. He peeked in on Elizabeth. Though she had dressed, she was sound asleep across her rumpled bed. She snored—gusty little snores. He smiled and took a place outside her door with his Sharps and his Winchester at his feet and the Colt in his lap. Cocked his Stetson over his eyes and was asleep in seconds.

He was in the black for several hours, his body hurrying to make up for yesterday's wear and tear.

The scream woke him, it startled him so. He

jumped to his feet, kicking his Sharps halfway across the car, and the Colt was in his hand seeking a target as the scream rang and settled down.

Elizabeth was at the door. "John, what?"

"I don't know. Get your gun."

Somebody—it sounded like Nelsh—was calling, "Is everybody all right? Who's hurt?"

The scream was the sound of terrible torment, a scream beyond pain. It was the scream of a soul at its first glimpse of Hell.

"John?" the trembling voice called. "John, they got me!"

Slocum had his pocket watch up to the light. Near five-thirty. Sun'd be coming up in another half hour or so.

"John, it's your old pal Jake. John, you wouldn't believe what these bastards are doing to me!"

Slocum called, "Anybody see anything? Anything at all?"

Though every man was awake and everyone searched the plains, nobody saw a living being.

Jake's voice went on. Sometimes it used words, sometimes it just screamed.

Elizabeth stood beside Slocum. "John, we simply must do something."

"We stay put," he said.

The agonized voice begged John Slocum for help. He spoke about knives and the flaying of skin. "They're enjoyin' it, John! Please—help me!"

Elizabeth put her hands over her ears and ran back into the car.

At least Slocum was rested some. "Everybody keep their eyes peeled," he said. "When they can't get us to come out after them, they'll come after us.

Don't pay no mind to Jake. Ain't nothin' anybody can do for him now."

Jake thought otherwise. His entreaties continued for a long time, punctuated by screams. Hope was slow to fade. He knew help was near; he just knew it.

Nelsh was hanging over the cab trying to see better. "Isn't there anything we can do?"

"Sure," Slocum said angrily. "We can go out there and get shot up, and all the wounded'll be sounding like Jake by midday. We can join Jake, but we can't save him. Hell, that's what they're hoping we'll do."

"I thought you didn't know Apaches."

Slocum spat. "I know Indians."

Jake alternately screamed and begged for an eternity that wasn't so very long by the clock. Slocum paced back and forth nervously, warning his alert men for the fight.

Jake's last words were remarkably clear, remarkably ordinary. "It's Welfleet done this to me, John. He's enjoyin' it as much as the Apaches are." His final shriek made the hair stand on end as Jake's soul made its welcome migration from the tortured body.

Briskly, Jay Nelsh walked to the flatcar, where most of the fighters were gathered, rifle muzzles poked through the timbers.

"Where's your rifle, Nelsh?"

"Oh, hell, John. What good would it do me? I'm no marksman."

"You can always use it on yourself. If Jake . . ."

He waved the suggestion away. "No, no. I'd fumble that too. John, who does Welfleet want dead?"

In a moment the sun would pop up and Slocum

could fire a quirly. He'd been dying for a smoke all night and he wondered whether he'd have time to finish it before the Apaches killed him.

"I am Welfleet's enemy. The rest of you are simply incidental," Nelsh said.

First the sun. "Steady, men." Slocum had the quirly all ready. When the shadows were gone, he'd fire it up. To Nelsh he said, "He can't let anybody live now. Nobody."

Nelsh jumped up on the top of the pile of ties and shouted, "Welfleet! I want to talk to you. I'll give you what you want!"

"Get down off there!" Slocum made a grab for Nelsh's leg, but the man danced away.

"You can have me, Welfleet, if you let the others go!"

Any second Slocum expected a bullet to take Nelsh off the ties. Any moment. He lunged again and bashed his hand, quite destroying his quirly. "Get down from there, you idiot!"

Miraculously, no bullet came. Maybe the Apaches were surprised, or maybe Welfleet was sick of killing. Geronimo was probably curious.

The tension drained out of Slocum's body. He closed his eyes, opened them. Nelsh was still up there. He had his hands on his hips. With a shaking hand, Slocum rolled himself another quirly. Might as well get some good from this interruption.

"I mean what I say, Welfleet! You can have the damn railroad. I got a daughter, Welfleet, and she's worth more to me than the Great Northern. She's worth my life and more."

The smoke curled into Slocum's lungs and set him into a fit of coughing.

The sun threw odd silhouettes on the rough railroad ties.

"Why should I trade you anything, Nelsh?" Damned if it wasn't Senator Welfleet himself.

"You may be able to take us, Welfleet, but it won't come cheap. We'll be looking for you! How about your allies? Is there any Apache who wants to talk?"

Though it was very soft, everybody heard the sound—the faint, soft, murderous chuckle.

Welfleet hollered, "The Apaches talk with their knives, Jay."

"Slocum, I'm going out. I want you to accompany me."

Without further ado, Jay Nelsh jumped off the car and marched manfully across the bare plains.

The sun was at his back, making him look bigger and brighter than a man should look. The surprise protected him.

It was Slocum's job, after all. With a curse, he dropped onto the roadbed. He could feel that sharp gravel right through his boots.

John Slocum had a hundred complaints to address to the man but when he caught up and joined his insane march into nothingness, he didn't dare say a word for fear his voice would break.

A slight smile played on Nelsh's lips. "John, I'm glad you could join me."

"Sure."

They passed two Apaches lying spread out beside small patches of cover that couldn't have hidden a ground squirrel. The Apaches followed Nelsh and Slocum with their guns.

"Don't move real quick," Slocum said. It was a

chilly morning but the sweat ran off his forehead into his eyes and stung. He didn't wipe it away.

Not a hundred yards from the ambushed train, the ground dropped into a hollow, perhaps two hundred feet across and twenty feet from lip to sump. Thick-stemmed marsh grasses grew in the bottom. For some of the year there was water here, anyway.

Slocum saw Jake hanging from a single pole. His head was thrown back in agony. The agony was more apparent without scalp or cheeks.

Three Indians, a filthy Senator Welfleet, and Geronimo himself. Slocum's boots went pit, pit, pit in the dirt and tiny clouds of white dust billowed. The ground was real alkaline in this country, he'd heard. Most of the dry-weather springs were bad. He raised one hand in the peace gesture, wishing he'd brought his Winchester. There were more Apaches than he had bullets in his Colt.

Slocum didn't speak the Apache lingo, of course, but he'd lived with the Blackfeet long enough to pick up Piegan, Crow, and a smattering of Ree. The sign language's symbols were universal among all plains Indians. Slocum signed for a parley, hoping he could arrange a truce before Nelsh promised complete surrender.

"I speak your tongue," Geronimo interrupted. "Do you speak Chiricahua?"

"I have never been in your country," Slocum said.

"This man," Nelsh interrupted, "says you are men of honor."

Geronimo stared before he burst into laughter. It wasn't his low, murderous chuckle; it sounded more like crows cackling furiously. The other pair of Indians didn't laugh aloud, but they stretched their mouth lines into a humorous arrangement.

The other Indians joined them, one on the left, another on the right, and Slocum sensed at least one more behind them.

"We have killed more Apache than I had thought," Slocum said.

No telling how they'd take that. Slocum swallowed, but he was ready to die. Once again Geronimo laughed. These two white men said the funniest things.

Slocum was beginning to think the whole thing was pretty funny too. "Why do you fight for this . . ." he indicated the senator with a gesture of unspeakable contempt, contempt so strong he could not name the man.

"He will send us home," Geronimo said. "He will send all my people home."

"Oh, my," Slocum said. The laughter boiled up in his throat then, and it was just as fierce as Geronimo's laughter, and quite as mad. He laughed until the tears ran from his eyes and his sides hurt. He laughed until he sputtered to a stop. "You believe that . . . that . . ." The laughter came again.

Geronimo looked at the scruffy, fat senator, and the smile came to his cruel lips. And Geronimo laughed, his laughter joining Slocum's, and two voices rang across the plains. "Oh, yes," he laughed. "we believed him. . . ."

The senator went into his coat pocket for a pistol, which he aimed at Jay Nelsh.

That sobered everybody. Quite reasonably, John Slocum said, "Welfleet, if you kill Nelsh, I'll drop you. A slug or two into me won't stop me. You ever seen a man kill once he was dead?''

"I have seen such a thing myself,'' Geronimo noted.

"God damn it,'' the senator said, "kill them! Kill them both!''

Everything hung in the balance and could have gone either way.

Jay Nelsh said, "The fight is between me and the senator. As men of honor, you must permit me to fight my enemy.''

Slocum struck like a snake, batting the senator's pistol down as he pulled the trigger. The report was loud for a short gun and the powder flash around the cylinder burned Slocum's hand. He twisted the weapon back against Welfleet's thumb, tugged, and it came away in his hand. He hurled the pistol very far into the distance.

The balance had shifted. Welfleet's move was a bad mistake. Geronimo crossed his arms. He was having a hell of a time. "A man's enemies are his own,'' he announced.

Slocum turned to Nelsh. "You can fight him if you want. Any special way you want to kill him?''

"I'm no good with a gun.''

"Knife? Hatchet?''

"I don't know.''

Slocum scratched his cheek. "If you want to please your audience, you'll fight with knives.''

"Well, I'm not fighting,'' Welfleet said, "Knives!'' He shuddered.

"I guess there's your answer,'' Slocum said. "Slice him up like a buffalo hump.''

Nelsh had no scruples, and no skill either. Geron-

imo threw his sharp blade at the railroad baron's feet
and another Indian handed the senator a long, slightly
curved blade with an ebony handle.

Slocum stepped back to coach. "You ever fence
before? Ever gut an animal?"

"No" to both questions. Nelsh had never been in
the army and had never used a saber either.

"At least you don't know any mistakes." Slocum
advised Nelsh in a whisper. Nobody was showing
Senator Welfleet a damn thing. He'd set his knife on
the ground and walked away from it.

"Shuck off your shirt, wrap it around your arm.
It'll make a bad wound if you get stabbed through it
anyway."

Nelsh was sinewy, but he didn't have much mus-
cle on him. "Use your left hand to feint and keep
him guessing. When you get close, try for his throat.
That's where you'll kill him best. Or the kidneys—
right here in the small of the back." Slocum patted
the spot on Nelsh's back.

The Indians formed a circle twenty feet across.
Slocum whispered, "Stay cool. Stab, don't slash.
Remember, he's just as scared as you are."

Nelsh cocked an eyebrow. "Scared? I'm not scared
at all." As instructed, he marched resolutely toward
the senator with his knife before him, a little awkward but full of determination.

The senator's hands were palms out. "Jay, this
isn't the white man's way to settle problems."

Nelsh might have reminded him of the death he'd
caused, the danger to his daughter, his murderous
allies, but the time for talking was past. He stabbed
Senator Welfleet through the flesh of his hand.

The senator screamed, not as loud as Jake had but with real feeling.

Crab-like, he scuttled after his own knife and grabbed it. "Jay," he puffed, "this isn't reasonable. Jay!"

When the senator stumbled against the Indians, they pushed him back into the circle, and they took very great pleasure in doing it. The two men who'd ridden his pursuit train with him pushed a little harder.

Nelsh chased the puffing senator around the ring. Suddenly the senator charged, striking down like a hammer blow. Nelsh blocked the blade with his arm but the knife was razor-sharp and sliced through to find blood. The sight of blood cheered the senator considerably. Besides, he was on the offensive, pursuing his enemy. "Ah-ha," he cried. "Ah-ha!"

Nelsh waited until the senator's guard was down and pushed his knife suddenly into the senator's stomach. When he pulled it back, the senator released a little fart sound from the new hole in his abdomen. "Oh," he said. "Oh, Jesus." He covered the hole with his hand. "Don't," he said.

But Jay Nelsh did. He'd never killed a man before and he wasn't exactly sure where to stab and where to cut, and the senator did keep his hands up over his throat, but Nelsh was willing to do the job, standing in close, stabbing, slashing at whatever parts of his enemy he could reach. He slashed the senator's arms and hands to the bone and stabbed him in the gut a dozen times. Both men were covered with blood when the senator fell to his knees, crawling blindly away. Nelsh jumped on his back and stabbed for the small of the back, for the kidneys. He rode Senator Welfleet into the dirt, stabbing.

Jay Nelsh rose, dazed. His lips moved. He held the knife ready to stab.

"Jay!" Slocum cried. "Give the man of honor his knife."

Jay Nelsh was just smart enough to wipe Geronimo's knife clean of blood and extend it butt first.

"You have learned," Geronimo said. "You are old to be learning, but you have learned.".

An Apache sawed at Welfleet's scalp. Technically, the scalp belonged to Nelsh, but Slocum signed quickly that the senator's scalp would be bad medicine for whites.

"We are done with each other," Geronimo announced. "He promised to bring my people back to their mountains."

Nelsh walked back toward the train. He was walking like a weary man, but he'd make it all right.

"Welfleet lied. His kind always lies."

Geronimo smiled. "He won't lie again. Where is my country?"

Slocum pointed to the south.

"How far?"

Slocum scratched his head. The heat of the new sun felt good on his shoulders. "A thousand—fifteen hundred miles?"

Geronimo let a look of disappointment cross his face. "That is very far."

"Yeah," Slocum said. "They tell me Apaches are great runners."

J. D. HARDIN

"THE MOST EXCITING WESTERN WRITER SINCE LOUIS L'AMOUR"
—JAKE LOGAN